Terror-organisation
The Dawn of the True Islam and the real IRA

Hannah Elisa Walsh

Terror-organisation The Dawn of the True Islam and the real IRA

Aspekt Publishers

Terror-organisation The Dawn of the True Islam and the real IRA

© Hannah Elisa Walsh
© 2017 Aspekt Publishers
Amersfoortsestraat 27, 3769 AD Soesterberg, Nederland
info@uitgeverijaspekt.nl-http://www.uitgeverijaspekt.nl

Coverdesign: Imad Loukili
Internals: Mariska Rooth

ISBN: 9789463380966
NUR: 300

All rights reserved. No part of this book may be reproduced, stored in a retrieval system, or transmitted in any form or by any means, electronic, electrostatic, magnetic tape, mechanical, photocopying, recording or otherwise, without the written permission of the publisher: Uitgeverij Aspekt, Amersfoortseweg 27, 3769 AD Soesterberg, Nederland.

Preface

"Bionn cluasa ar na clathacha"
Irish proverb: the walls do have ears.

For all victims of terrorism. With gratitude I think back to the magic time I had in Ireland, the lovely Irish people which gave me so much inspiration, the magnificent landscape and the wonderful Irish music.

Hannah Elisa Walsh

1.

'Allahu akbar.' 'Allahu akbar.' Siobhan woke up with a start. She couldn't get used to the early shouting of the prayers in Arabic. She felt disoriented for a moment, but there was no time to lose. Today she had a lot to do. She had the luxury to have a tent of her own. The other fighters in training had to share their tent with six other men. Siobhan took the shouting to Allah for granted, if she could get the right military training her goal would be reached. That goal was learning how to commit a terror attack with precision. Her organisation, the real IRA, had donated a little fortune to pay for her training in the desert. Siobhan put on her uniform and walked to a tent where she could wash herself. She threw a splash of water on her face and observed herself in a mirror divided in two by a crack. Reddish hair, her light skin which wasn't made for the sunshine of the desert, was covered with red spots all over now. She realized that in a short period her whole outlook would be changed completely, another colour of hair, a pair of glasses on her nose and with special make up. A totally different appearance would be the result. Her spoken English had to be transformed into an upper class British accent. Siobhan longed for the end of her heavy training in the desert, and the start of her mission at last. Her breakfast was ready when she came back to her tent. It was not allowed to sit with the men behind the table, but she couldn't care less. The only one she spoke to directly was her female translator Lailah. She was taking care of the translation for all the instructions of the training. Lailah and Shiobhan were the only women in the camp. They only had contact if necessary. Today she had to do a physical training and she would get an explanation about a secret weapon, or so she understood. Siobhan was not only curious but also wanted to learn new things. She looked at the entrance of the camp. It was formed by an opening in a wall made up of sandbags. On both sides to the entrance a black flag with white texts in Arabic was blowing in the wind. Siobhan had no idea what these texts meant, she did not care. The noise of the shouting in Arabic stopped, it was time to go to her training. She took up her regular place in the row. The man in front of the row started to shout out loud. Lailah stepped beside her and whispered in her ear that the men were given to hear that they had a greater goal in their lives; it was to obey Allah totally, establish his rule on earth and to live strictly by the rules of the Koran. Now it was time to start the physical training. Lailah motioned her that the first row had to move under the barbed wire, then climb over a fence, grab the gun and run with it a for a few rounds. Siobhan thought of green hills for a split second. Lailah gave her a hard push. It was time to move. She pushed her body under the barbed wire in the sand, and she grabbed her gun. A new command was given. Everybody had to stand in rows again. The first row had to start shooting at special targets.

Siobhan shot six times at the right spot. It gave her a feeling of satisfaction. Lailah motioned her to walk with her to a tent. She whispered in broken English that Siobhan would get an instruction about a secret weapon. The two women sat down in the tent. On the table lay a sort of little ball that had an unobtrusive grey tint. Lailah told her this was a prototype of a new weapon that was developed in a factory somewhere in the Yemen. A man entered the tent and sat down at the other end of the table. He was dressed in a grey uniform and had a dark brown turban on his head. A gun was hanging from his left shoulder. Siobhan heard the sound of the Arabic language which formed words. Lailah translated and said it was absolutely forbidden to speak with other people about this secret weapon, no matter what. She had to understand it was a big favour that she got an explanation about the use of it. But that was not the only thing. She was chosen to test the weapon for the first time and had to understand this was a big privilege, too. The man took the little ball in his hands. With his thumb he touched a small black spot. You could hear a soft click. The man demonstrated that you had to either throw away the little weapon or put it down somewhere; this depended on the target at hand. Lailah explained that it would spread a gas mixture which could not be smelled in any way. It would kill all life around: humans, animals and plants in a matter of moments. The little ball would evaporate and vanish totally after it had spread its poison, and no one would ever be able to trace it. The man produced a self-indulgent smile. The corners of Lailah's mouth went up, too. She told Siobhan again that it was strictly forbidden to talk about this, especially when she would be captured. If the silence was broken, the penalty would be death. The network could trace her anywhere on the world, no doubt about it.

2.

Ann Pigden had overslept this Monday morning. Every Monday they played petanque in the park, with the same participants, at the same time as a sort of routine. With great haste she put on her shorts. It was going to be a very warm day again. Her partner Lucy was busy in their small but comfortable kitchen, in the chalet which they had bought five years ago. Ann loved to live in a sort of English village in a strange country. The park in the south of Portugal reminded her of the time she was living in a British compound in Germany. She had served as an officer in the British army in West-Germany after the Second World War. This park was mainly populated by British pensionados, a few Scottish families and lately a few Dutch families. They had bought a chalet, too, to celebrate their vacations in the Algarve. Ann despised the free mentality of the few Dutch neighbours she had. In her eyes they had no feeling for law and order at all. She brushed her teeth and looked in the mirror. She saw her own tired face. She had had one of her devastating nightmares again. The bullet she had fired off pierced the head of a boy, his eye was pushed out of his head. The blood was streaming from the hole and it just never stopped. Most of the time Ann woke up sweating and got up to take a sleeping pill, hoping she would fall into a dreamless sleep. 'Ann, would you like to have a cup of tea?', Lucy asked. 'I also made some toast for you'. 'Yes, I would like to have a cup of tea and a slice of toast. I must hurry to be in time for our game of petanque. Are you coming to watch us play?' "I don't know yet Ann, I want to clean the house first,' Lucy replied. Ann drank her tea quickly and put a piece of toast in her mouth. She picked up her little petanque balls and left their spacious chalet, which was on a double plot. They had chosen a double plot, which was more expensive. They had to pay more rent every year, but they lived here permanently and also wanted to have a bigger garden because of their dog, Djinx. It could run around freely on his three legs. Ann wiggled slowly towards the petanque field which was behind a row of other chalets. Some were spacious, some were a bit smaller, with little gardens. Every garden was decorated with flowers and different palm trees. Some had pots with oleander, bougainvillea and cacti next to the porch. When you passed you couldn't avoid greeting people who were sitting in the garden or on their decking. 'Good morning Jeff, are you coming to play petanque?,' Ann asked. 'I am sorry, I can't be there today, I don't feel well at all.' 'That's a pity Jeff, I hope you'll feel better soon.' 'Jeff,' Ann thought, probably he'd drunk too much cheap whiskey again. If he goes on like this, he'll drink himself to death.' She wiggled along the chalet of Maddy. 'Hi Maddy, are you walking with me?' 'Yes, but I need to grab my stuff first.' She entered the chalet Maddy had carefully decorated with her husband, Graham. Their lives in Portugal had been perfect until the day cancer was detected in her body. Now she had to fly up and down to the UK ever so often, since she didn't trust the Portuguese doctors, although in general the health care was pretty good in Portugal.

Everybody in the park knew this. When they arrived at the petanque field some people were already there. They all hugged each other. On the edge of the group stood a blonde woman with blue eyes, she was new in the park. The British looked at her with suspicion, since she was one of the Dutch who had recently bought a chalet from the owner of the park. He had confiscated the chalet from a British family that couldn't afford the yearly rent anymore. The blonde woman opened her mouth. With a heavy Dutch accent she introduced herself as Paula van Walsum. She asked if she could play along. The British agreed reluctantly. Now the game could start. While playing the latest gossip went the round: about who had which disease, who had to go back to the UK and also the latest news about Fausto, the Portuguese owner of the park. Everybody hated him. To them he was an exploiter who wanted to take as much money from the innocent British citizen as possible. Ann couldn't concentrate on anything very well this morning. Her balls were missing their target, while her bullet never missed when she was serving in the army. She felt annoyed and apologized for her bad game. When they were finished everybody sat down at the terrace of the small restaurant which overlooked the swimming pool. With great effort the park residents convinced Fausto to place handrails at the stairs of the swimming pool. Finally, after two years they were installed, the wrong ones in the eyes of the residents, but you couldn't have it all, could you? The poor Portuguese could not help they didn't understand the high standards of the UK, it was above their level. When everybody was seated the group expected the cook, an elderly Portuguese lady, to serve them at once. In the end, they were the ones who brought in the money in the park. Paula van Walsum tried to start a conversation with Ann. 'It's really nice, Ann, that you play every week, I understood you also have a charity market every month?' 'Yes, we do', Ann replied. 'We try to sell as much as possible for a children's home here in the neighbourhood, the Portuguese can pay for their education, but not much else, you see.' 'Oh no,' Ann thought: 'Why in heavens' name does that Dutch woman want to talk to me?'. Maddy looked at the entrance of the restaurant and wondered why Augusta hadn't arrived yet to serve them. Augusta just appeared. In her poor English she asked what everyone would like to drink and eat. The British always complained about the poor English of the Portuguese people, but not one of them really bothered to learn decent Portuguese. Ann was one of the few people who went to lesson every week. She thought that she had to learn the language of the country where she lived. During the period she was stationed in Germany she had learned to speak and write German. Ann ordered a tuna salad. She tried to loose weight since her overweight gave her a lot of trouble in the hot climate of Portugal. The blonde woman tried to chat with her again. 'We are so happy with our wonderful chalet here in the park. We even have a private swimming pool! Do you live here permanently?', she asked. 'Yes, we do', Ann replied. She turned her head and took a bite from her salad. A headache struck her. 'Excuse me, I don't feel very well, I didn't sleep very well last night.' 'Would you like me to walk with you, Ann?', Maddy asked. 'No Maddy, it's okay, enjoy your lunch.' Ann grabbed her little balls, paid Augusta and wiggled herself down on the stairs. She shook her head while walking towards her chalet.

3.

first flashback
   Londonderry, 30th of January 1972.
   Seamus O'Connor looked at himself in the mirror. Today it was an important day. Today he participated in the peaceful demonstration against the British occupation of Northern Ireland. Yesterday they had had a secret meeting with the persons organising the march. They all agreed no form of violence would be used against the British. Dr. Martin Luther King was their role model: "We shall overcome someday". One day would see the liberation of Northern Ireland, one fine day in the not too distant future, when Catholics and Protestants would live in peace with one another. The children would walk without disturbance to school, totally safe. Northern Ireland would become a prosperous part of the Republic of Ireland. He felt immensely connected to the "The Northern Ireland Civil Rights Association". His wife Siobhan was scared, very scared that something would happen to him during the march, she had wished he would not participate at all. His little son of nine years old would like to join him, but this was out of the question. Seamus combed his hair, he would walk with nicely combed hair in the demonstration, and fight for justice. He ran down the stairs of their little house. His wife was sitting at the table, her son Brian on her lap. The light from outside shone through

the window and lit up a part of her face. Seamus looked at her and felt as if they were all in a painting together. He wiped a tear from his face. His son walked towards him and said: 'Dad.' Seamus lifted up his son and hugged him. His wife got up and gave him a cup of coffee. They were sitting silently at the kitchen table. 'My God, she is so beautiful,' he thought, looking at his wife. He kissed her, put on his cap and left the house. He knew a shortcut to the gathering place where the march would start. Everybody clapped each other on the shoulder to boost courage. Seamus felt happy to see all of his friends again. A long procession started to move in silence. His heart was beating fast. Suddenly he saw that his son one way or another had followed him. He grabbed his hand. The march proceeded; it was for freedom, for justice and for so much more.., for his son who once would live in peace. Suddenly he heard shouting, he heard bullets were fired, he heard people screaming in pain. Then he felt an immense pain in his lower back. He fell on the ground. His son Brian bent over him, but within a split second he was grabbed by another man. The man ran away, away from the gunfire to shelter behind a wall. It was safe there. Little Brian shouted: 'Dad, dad, dad.' Liam carried Brian home on his back. He knocked on the door, and Siobhan opened. She knew already by intuition her husband was dead. She embraced Brian. They heard more gunfire in the distance. Siobhan said: 'When does this ever stop?' She touched Brian's hair. He began to cry. 'Where is my dad? Where is daddy?'. Liam and Siobhan went silent.

4.

Ann watched the BBC. One of the good things of the park was that you could receive all British television channels very well through the dishes that were placed beside every chalet. She really enjoyed to watch programmes about the history of the UK, at the time it still was the centre of a great empire. It was the time when the British culture and the English language were dominant. 'We can all see what a mess India became since we left,' she thought. 'The people should be thankful to us, because we brought civilisation, education and economic growth. The position of women and girls in Indian society has gone from bad to worse since we left.' Yesterday she read about a group that raped a girl in India. 'Those men have no idea about good and evil. Most people live like rats in the streets. Horses are treated like a piece of shit over there,' Ann thought. She heard the clock beating seven times. The BBC news started. Another scandal with a media tycoon, another sex scandal, where was the decent country of her past? She walked to the telly to switch it off. While standing very close to the television an item about the troubles was announced. Ann froze totally and sat down again to watch. It was about an investigation of the killing of an Irishman in Derry, back in 1972. The news item was about the fact that despite the investigation, the circumstances of his death were never brought to light. A huge report appeared about Bloody Sunday, David Cameron made his excuses to the Irish people. Ann shook her head, when would this ever stop?

For the Irish it was never enough. Why didn't they let the past rest in peace? No one would benefit if they didn't. Northern Ireland was prosperous now, with a good economic growth, and Belfast a flourishing city nowadays. More and more international companies opened up their doors, there was a brand new shopping mall. No bombs exploded every week anymore. People just wanted to move on with their lives and did not want to dwell on the past every day. Ann could not understand that the Orange marches were held every year, as these were a danger to the status quo. Strange guys the Irish, why in heaven's name would you like to walk as a protestant through a catholic neighbourhood, with the sole purpose of provoking the other community? What people can do to each other. Ann shook her head and turned off the television. Lucy would soon return from her weekly group, where they played cards together. The door of their chalet was opened. 'Hi Ann, I'm back,' Lucy said. "Did you win?' Ann asked her. 'No, Jeff won. He is much too smart for me. That blonde Dutch woman was there again. She wanted to play with us. We felt obliged. Also, I heard that Fausto wants to modernize the park. And that he has in mind to raise the plot rent again!' 'What a pain in the ass this man is, he is taking advantage of us all the time. Can't we do something about this?' 'I don't know, Ann, I think it will become very difficult to get everyone on the same line to fight against Fausto.' 'Sit down Lucy, I'll make you a cup of tea.' Ann wiggled to the kitchen. Then she walked back to Lucy and kissed her on the mouth. 'I still love you Lucy,' she said. 'Even after all that has happened?' 'Yes, you always supported me.' Ann looked through the window. She shuddered, it was cold for this time of year in the Algarve, most of the time in April they could already sit outside on the veranda in the evening. 'I watched the BBC news, there was an item about the troubles, just before I wanted to turn off the TV. 'Nothing new I hope?' 'They keep on digging in the past, but for what?' 'The standard of living is very good in Northern Ireland at the moment, and thanks to us they have very good social security. They should be grateful for being part of the UK.' 'That is exactly my idea, Lucy, let's stop talking about this and not waste more of our precious time on the subject. Let us drink a glass of wine in the restaurant.' 'Yes, let's do that, it may distract us a bit. Maybe Jeff, Maddy and Nelson will be there, too.' Ann and Lucy put on their coats and took their flashlights. The road to the restaurant was very dark. The entrance to the restaurant was a heavy curtain that separated the bar and the restaurant from the outside world. It was as if you were part of a secret society. 'Hi, how you are you both today?' 'Great to have you here this evening,' Nelson said. 'We are fine Nelson, but how are you?' 'I keep myself going that's all. Did you know that Diana is doing very bad?' 'She is getting the best treatment in the hospital in Faro, but the treatment does not give positive results at all. Tomorrow I have to go to the hospital again, would you mind watching Bobby for a while?' Bobby wagged his little tail, he knew Ann and Lucy very well. 'No problem,

Nelson, don't worry, you know he is always welcome at our place,' Ann said. Nelson knew very well he needed his fellow park residents, not only to give him the feeling he was part of a community, but also to help him with practical things sometimes. He loved the park, how it was situated, its mainly British population, and his life after retirement. He used to have a good job with Shell, from which he felt liberated now. He and his wife Diana had agreed very quickly to sell their big house in London and to buy the chalet in the Algarve. They really enjoyed their lives in Portugal, until Diana got intestinal cancer. Nelson felt angry sometimes. Why in heaven's name Diana? She was a lovely person, who did not only help other people, but she set up a programme to raise money for cats and dogs that were neglected. In Portugal a lot of dogs and cats were living in the streets, and nobody cared about their fate. 'Can I offer you a drink, Nelson?' Lucy asked. 'Yes, a pint please, you know my brand.' She walked towards the bar. Cilia was on duty this evening. Oh no, Lucy thought, she doesn't speak a word of English, now I need to speak Portuguese to her again, which I don't like at all since I only know a few words.' 'One beer please, and two glasses of white wine.' She pointed at the brand Nelson drank. Knowing better, Cilia started a conversation in Portuguese with Lucy. Lucy nodded from time to time. She didn't want to look impolite. Cilia filled two glasses with white wine and opened a bottle of beer. She looked at her watch, she still had to work until 10.30 PM, which meant a shift of more than ten hours. Sometimes she got so tired of being friendly to the English all the time. At home she had to run a household as well. Although her husband was unemployed, he did not care less about doing something in their home. He tried to earn a little something by going to the beach and catch little crabs. The crabs were on the menu of the more expensive restaurants in the neighbourhood. Nelson drank his beer, he was thirsty. He always was when he became angry at the thought of Diana's cancer. Lucy said, as if she guessed his thoughts: 'It must be very difficult for you to see your lovely Diana being wrecked by such a terrible disease. Sometimes life seems to be so full of injustice. Such a lovely person like her falling so ill. I don't understand life, Nelson.' 'Me neither Lucy,' Nelson replied. Diana tried to live as healthy as she possibly could, she didn't smoke, hardly drank any alcohol. She was looking very beautiful for her age and she always was busy helping other people. 'Yes I know, we all like her very much. Sometimes I wonder if God is righteous at all. Why her?' 'I don't know, Lucy, why some people have more luck than others, you can run into an accident, or your plane may fall from the sky, life is by its nature not fair. "Why are you talking about such sad subjects?,' Ann asked. She felt that she had to say something, too. 'Let's think in a positive way, perhaps Diana will get cured from her illness, so cheers and let us drink another one.' The curtain opened. Jeff entered with a cigarette in his mouth. Cilia motioned he had to put out the cigarette immediately. 'Hi everybody, it's great seeing you all.' 'We are discussing the serious things of life, Jeff.' 'What could be serious under the Portuguese sun?' 'Life is one big party altogether!' 'Perhaps for some people, Jeff, we were talking about the situation of Diana, the latest news about her is not good at all.' 'I am sorry to hear that, Nelson, I didn't

know this. I wish you a lot of strength, old chap.'
'It's okay, you couldn't know.' Jeff ordered a pint. He walked towards one of the little tables that were covered with dirty white table cloths. Everybody in the park wondered where the expensive yearly plot rent went. For sure it was not spent on fixing the restaurant, or painting the terrace. For years and years now the residents of the park were promised there would be made improvements in the park, but nothing had happened so far. Fausto tried to reduce the costs concerning the park as much as possible. Stories were told about him, he couldn't order anything anymore without paying up front, in cash. It was said he was on a blacklist, since he never paid the bills of his suppliers. The permanent residents of the park were totally dependent on the ever changing rules of the park. They had nowhere else to go, their house in the UK had been sold.

Ann told Lucy she was tired and wanted to go home. She hoped she would be able to sleep the coming night.

5.

Brian bent over the cradle. He looked at his sleeping daughter Siobhan. She seemed to be totally at peace. His wife Lilly had given birth a few days before. She still felt very weak. His mother in law, Deirdre, helped her as much as she could. She cooked, cleaned the house, took care of the baby and laid her at the breast of her mother. Brian felt proud, but also sad, he missed his father, especially after the birth of his first child. He wished for his father so much to hold his granddaughter in his arms. It wasn't meant to be. Brian thought about his father every day. His good father, who was brutally torn out of his life. He wanted to push away these thoughts, but he didn't succeed. His mother never remarried. She could hardly cope with the loss of her husband. Her family had tried to help her but she didn't regain her lust for life. She suffered from melancholy and everyone thought she would die of sadness. Brian heard a sound from outside, as if someone had thrown something against a wall. He ran downstairs and opened the door. He saw that a few rotten tomatoes and a dead bird were laying in his front yard. It was an omen, a sign of what could happen the coming period, when the Orange marches would pass right through the catholic neighbourhood. For sure the Orangemen wouldn't leave this part of Belfast alone. It was 1988, when would this ever stop? Would his daughter be the next generation that had to grow up with hatred between protestants and catholics in Belfast ? Would she be fearful of more bombs exploding in the city? The Orangemen had to keep up a long tradition. The origin of their heritage dated back to the time of the Glorious Revolution, in the year 1688. The protestant William of Orange, William III took the power from the catholic James II. In this way the protestant faith was secured, also in the north of Ireland. The Ulster treaty prevented that Ulster could become a part of the free catholic Irish Republic, the Orangemen carried this with them in their genes. They had no plans whatsoever to give up their privileged economic position in Northern Ireland in the present, no way. Brian and his family had to settle for a small house in a poor neighbourhood. He was glad he had a simple job with a low salary. Brian didn't feel like going to the police to report the incident with the dead bird. It was no use, the ones who did this would never be caught. He knew this from experience. Tomorrow he had to go to the small office of the insurance company again. The whole day he was busy putting data of clients into a system. The work had no challenge for him, but at least he had a job. He wondered if he would be able to give his daughter a proper education. Maybe she had to leave school early to look for a job. He hoped there would be not more incidents when he was away at work tomorrow. He hoped that the Orange marches wouldn't cause so much trouble this year, but there was a big chance that they would. Just like last year they would pass in front of his door. Some people probably couldn't resist this. Action, reaction, violence answered by violence. Strange that religion could lead to hating each other so much... to wanting to kill each other instead of respecting each other's views. He felt cold, and shuddered.

6.

'Please forward your passport, together with your ticket,' a voice from the speakers said. Siobhan took her passport from the inner pocket of her coat. She had to get used to the sounds of daily life, colours and certain areas after her period in the desert. Before she was leaving for Amsterdam, she had spent the night in a hotel near the Ben Gurion airport of Tel Aviv. The vibrant city with its positive and modern atmosphere, felt very pleasant. The beautiful boulevard along the beach with trendy cafés, disco's, women in colourful dresses, the different languages she heard; English, Hebrew, Portuguese, French and Russian, gave her a feeling of happiness for a moment. Sometimes she heard Arabic. Then her shoulder made a spontaneous movement as if it wanted to salute automatically. Siobhan looked at her new fake British passport and she smiled. She stared at the photo and her new name: Donnah Nugent, with modern glasses and dark brown hair. She picked up her luggage and lined up to pass the ticket control before she could enter the plane. Two stewardesses with blue outfits, decked with the KLM logo, were standing beside a gate. They were talking in Dutch, Siobhan heard a lot of the hard 'ch' sound, she couldn't understand a word of what they were saying. She held her passport with her photo showing towards one of them. The ground stewardess looked at it very carefully and said: 'Have a nice trip to Amsterdam, I hope you enjoy your stay in Holland.' Her second test of the new identity had passed. The first test at entering Israel without being noticed had been her baptism of fire. When the Israelis were suspicious one way or another concerning a certain person entering Israel, this person was taken away to a separate room for interrogation. It also included being frisked with a special digital secret system. If the authorities thought the person might be a threat to the security of the country he or she was held in custody for as long as it was necessary; or it could mean refusal to enter the country altogether. Siobhan entered Israel without problems from Jordan, with her new identity. In all probability, she seemed like a person of no importance. And this was exactly how it should be. She walked with her trolley to the entrance of the plane. Her seat was situated near a window. She asked the young man who was already sitting to stand up so that she could pass, she heard that he had a British accent. This could be a good opportunity to test her new accent. He introduced himself as David Lewis. 'Donnah Nugent, nice to meet you.' Siobhan wanted to say something more to test her pronunciation. 'What a lovely city Tel Aviv is, don't you think so?' 'I really enjoyed the beach and the boulevard. It has such a wonderful atmosphere.' 'You were on vacation in Israel?' Siobhan thought for a second about a good answer to this. 'I visited a friend of mine.' 'Well, what a coincidence, I visited a friend of mine whom I hadn't seen for a long time.' Indeed, it is a coincidence, Siobhan said to herself. She thought why in heaven's name does he fly to Amsterdam and not directly to London? As if David guessed her thoughts he said; 'I am visiting Amsterdam, just a weekend before I have to go back to London to start working again.' 'What kind of work do you do?' 'I am working in the City.' 'What are you doing yourself, do you also work in London?' 'Oh well, I work as special needs teacher in the northern part of London.' 'Not an easy area to work in,' David said. A stewardess passed by. She asked if they wanted to read a newspaper, she had the Times and a few other papers. Siobhan wanted to read a newspaper, to end the conversation with David, who thought she was from London. There was probably no Northern Irish accent in her English anymore. She took the newspaper, and pretended she was very interested in the main article about another eavesdropping scandal in the British media. 'Let them destroy each other,' she thought when she had read it. She turned the page and looked at an article that said that the international Islamic terrorism was getting more and more extreme. The article said there was a link with some Muslim groups in the UK. This problem was denied by many, the writer of the article wrote, and he claimed there was a bomb lying beneath the surface of British society. Most politicians and important scientists had no answer whatsoever. 'Maybe they are right,' Siobhan thought. She folded the newspaper and closed her eyes. She hoped she could get some sleep. In Amsterdam there was an intensive training waiting for her. It was mostly psychology, if she would be able to withstand interrogation of any kind. For ten minutes she was deep asleep, freed from all thoughts and nightmares. She just heard some noises far off. After a while she opened her eyes. She looked through the window outside and had no idea which country they were flying over, but for sure it was a beautiful country with mountains and a long seashore. Maybe it was Italy, the country with the great treasures of art, and the history of the Roman Empire. During her high school she once saw a travel guide about Italy, with beautiful city squares, museums and a photo of the statue of David by Michelangelo, the very impressive square of Saint Peter and the Sistine Chapel. She had asked her father if they could travel to Italy to see all of that with their own eyes. Her father explained to her this was impossible for 'our kind of people', meaning it would be much too costly for them. She felt very disappointed, but she promised herself one thing : one day I will visit Rome and look at the David with my own eyes and secretly try to touch him. She closed her eyes. She imagined that she was walking on the beach along the seashore that was now below her, her feet in the fine sand. Sand, sand, sand she had felt this everywhere for the last few months in the desert, in her clothes, her notebooks, her sleeping bag. Endless sand dunes everywhere, with a burning sun above it. At nights the heaven was magnificent, with all the stars above. The nights had been full of an impressive silence, as opposed to the days with their noise of Arabic shouted out through the loudspeakers that were everywhere in the camp. The harsh regime, the heavy physical training, to learn to how to use weapons and the secret weapon, the loneliness she felt, she had coped with it to reach a higher goal. At last some justice, and a revenge for the senseless massacre of her people.

7.

Ann woke up suddenly in the middle of the night. She looked around frightened, and she was sweating heavily. The last image of her nightmare made her shudder. A man who collapsed before her eyes, the noise of the shooting, a boy who missed an eye, the blood which came out of the hole. The scene felt familiar, as if it was her steady partner during the night. Ann walked to the kitchen sink. She picked up a cup and filled it with water. In one gulp she drank all of it. She looked through the window, the moon was full, its light was shining on their well-organized garden. The flowers, bushes and trees were set up in a pattern, which gave her a feeling of order, and she loved this: order and clarity. This was the reason that she felt at home in the British army. The discipline and order, the clear commands and the hierarchy, to do your duty for the Queen and Great Britain, to serve a higher goal. Ann liked the fact that it was not necessary to ask herself critical questions about who she was and why she did things like she had done in her life. To answer those questions wasn't necessary at the time she served in the army. She really thought it had been very positive to represent her country abroad, especially in the time she was stationed in Germany. She had really enjoyed it, to be part of the allied forces at the time when it was still West-Germany. They were the counterweight against the great danger of aggressive communism with its origin in the Soviet Union. She did not just want to forget her stay in the time of the troubles in Northern Ireland, but also to suppress it completely, but she didn't succeed at all. Nothing had worked, nothing had helped, not even their emigration to this park in Portugal. Lucy had said that she had to seek help for her never ending nightmares and her sudden anxiety attacks. Ann didn't want to do this, she wanted to read a book, to play her games with others in the park and to cross the river with the little boat to Spain, where it was cheaper to do the groceries. She sat down in the big armchair and shut her eyes for a moment. Lucy had woken up, too, and felt the empty spot beside her. She stood up and walked to find her partner in the living room. There she saw Ann, breathing heavily in the armchair. She was muttering: 'Go away, eye, go away, eye.' Lucy shook Ann at her shoulders. 'What's the matter, Ann?' She realized it was a completely unnecessary question, she knew exactly what was going on, over and over again. 'I was dreaming again, but this time the dream was different. I saw a man lying on the floor, he was in pain. He turned towards me and looked me right in the eyes. He pointed at his wound in the lower part of his back. The blood was streaming out. He opened up his mouth and said: 'Why, why, why?'. 'This is an awful nightmare, Ann. You can't carry this any longer, you hardly sleep any more, you are exhausted. Tomorrow I'll make an appointment with father Steve of the Anglican church in Tavira. You are going to talk with him if you like it or not, period.' Ann realized there was no way out this time, she simply had to speak about the past to somebody she could trust. At least father Steve had a code of silence, in no way did she want anyone from the park to find out about her past. For sure people would hear that she was talking to father Steve and no doubt they would start to gossip. 'I will give it a thought, Lucy, you know how people are in the park. Please don't talk to anyone about this, no one must find out I was in the troubles, no one, otherwise we may just as well start to try and sell our chalet here, you know this.' 'Let us go outside to smoke a cigarette,' Lucy said. They put on their robes. Lucy opened the door to the large porch. They sat down in the rocking chair. The silence of the night felt as a relief. The moon overhead gave them a sense of peace in the tiny spot where they existed. In silence they smoked their cigarette.

8.

'Siobhan, are you coming downstairs, it's time to go to school.' Brian knew his daughter was very nervous. It was the season of the Orange marches again. Siobhan and some of her classmates had to walk through a protestant neighbourhood. Last time the children were spit at, their hair got torn at, and people had shouted at them : 'You wretched Catholics, bloody betrayers, terrorists, you should be banned to the Republic, get out now!'. Siobhan ran to the kitchen, but she did not feel like eating her breakfast at all. 'You need to eat, child, you can't go to school without eating, your father will see you to school, there is no need to be afraid,' her mother said. She picked up a comb and combed the beautiful red hair of Siobhan. She was very worried about her daughter; her face was very pale these days. She appeared to have a feeling for music. She probably inherited this from her grandfather, whom she had never known. He had played the pipes, the whistle and the violin. Siobhan just loved to play the violin. Brian sometimes played a traditional Irish song for her, Siobhan played it after him without any hesitation, her eyes closed. For sure she would play in one of the many groups that played Irish traditional music, played every week in the pubs. Perhaps she could become a music teacher. Lilly looked at the floor, they would never be able to afford a college education for their daughter. 'We're go-

ing', Brian said. He grabbed the hand of his daughter. 'Don't be afraid, I am with you all the time, whatever they shout at you, or throw at us, just move on and hold my hand.' With affection he looked at her face. He hoped his protection would be sufficient. They left the house together and walked to the end of the street. They had to turn right, walking through a dangerous area. Before they could turn right a group of men walked towards them. They carried orange flags and they had orange sashes around their big bellies. They started to shout the moment they noticed Brian and the children. 'You don't belong here, bugger off, you rats. Get a one way ticket to the Republic.' One of the men pushed Brian. Before he could get something out of his pocket, a police car arrived. The car had the flashlights on, and produced the intense sound of a siren. Four police officers stepped out of the car. This was an exception, not very often the police would intervene when there was trouble with the Orangemen. The officers stepped between the group of children, Brian and the Orangemen. Another car arrived. A photographer and a reporter got out and walked to Brian. A microphone was put in front of Brian's nose. 'What do you think of the Orangemen, sir?' One of the police officers motioned the reporter to go way. Brian could only say, in a split second : 'It's terrible all of this, in particular for our children.' The police officers accompanied the children and Brian, by walking next to them. One of them said in a typical Belfast accent : 'I feel so sorry for the children sir.' Siobhan, her friend Deirdre and Brian walked hand in hand to the entrance of the school, and then on to their classroom. Breda, their teacher, tried to hide her emotions, she felt happy that no one got wounded. When all the children got to their seats she said: 'Dear children, let's start with sing-

ing a song you all know from your grandmothers; Spancil hill. We will put our chairs in a circle and I'll get my violin.' She put her violin on her shoulder and started to play the melody of "Spancil Hill". Spontaneously the children began to sing along, they all knew the popular tune. After singing for about ten minutes Breda said: 'I am going to tell you a little story about the elves who are living near the lake of Killarney. When I am finished you can make a drawing about the story. Siobhan listened carefully to the story, her teacher was a wonderful storyteller. She could dream away for minutes on end. She saw the knotty old oaks standing in the misty weather, on the shore of the lake of Killarney and the clouds floating above the water. She could hear the birds sing, so vivid was her imagination. For a moment there was a complete silence. Breda had finished her story. The children were given paper and coloured pencils. They started drawing, and you could only hear the scratching on the paper. Breda smiled; she hoped the children could forget the hostility which had surrounded them this morning, if only for a few moments.

9.

The plane started its descent. They were flying through thick clouds now. It was raining. Siobhan loved the sight of this; rain and the beautiful shape of the swirling clouds. She had really missed this, clouds, rain and the fresh sea wind. In Belfast a lot of depressions passed, before going to Scotland. When the sun was shining for half an hour everybody said: 'It is a lovely sunny day!' After her high school period, which she had finished with high grades, she had left for the Republic of Ireland at once. She wanted to taste life before she committed herself to a longer period of studies. The first six months she was living in Dingle. She had found a room that did not cost much. During the evening and night she played her violin with a small group of musicians that played in one of the pubs of Dingle, which was very famous among the tourists, for the best Irish music. A lot of musicians from all over the world were coming to Dingle to play with the local musicians, to learn from them, and simply to have fun while playing. Siobhan met a lot of interesting people from all over the world, especially from Bretagne, the Celtic part in the west of France. She met young people from the USA, too, who wanted to know more about their roots. After her period in Dingle she went to Schull, on the Irish southern coast. Schull, an idyllic place near a beautiful bay, was surrounded by lush greenery. There were palm trees growing, fantastic native plants which were unique, all because of the mild climate and special circumstances on the green island. She had found a house to share with an American, who lived in Schull to paint and to find rest after a very hectic period in New York. Liza turned out to be a pleasant flatmate. Siobhan had worked as waitress in a small restaurant. During the summer a lot of tourists from the UK, the Netherlands and France visited Schull. The climate was very pleasant, and it had the most sunshine in all of Ireland. Beside her job as waitress she had a few private violin students who tried, with great effort, to learn to play the traditional music. A few of them were really talented and picked up the traditional melodies quite easily.

'What a lovely sight, the clouds and the rain, isn't it,' David said next to her. Siobhan looked at him; he was an attractive young man who obviously enjoyed the sight of the clouds and the falling rain. In normal circumstances she would have considered to exchange business cards, but now she thought it would be too risky. Suddenly David asked : 'Would you like to have dinner with me, this weekend? I know a very good Moroccan restaurant in the centre of Amsterdam, the food is awesome!' Siobhan thought for moment she was taking a risk by accepting the invitation, but on the other hand, why not? 'Yes, sure, I would like that, if you could just give me the address of the restaurant?' David gave her the address in writing. After the plane stopped and had arrived at its final destiny at Schiphol airport, David was so kind to get her trolley out of the overhead locker. The stewardess smiled kindly when they left the plane. Now the next test would come, to pass the Dutch border without any fuss. With her head up high she walked through the corridor, following the signs "Douane". 'What an enormous airport this is,' she thought. She had to walk at least fifteen minutes to arrive at the gate, to enter the Netherlands legally. The officer looked at the photo in her passport, looked at her and motioned that she could pass. She walked to the arrivals' hall. She would meet Sean and Samir. She had known Sean already for a long time, Samir she had never met before. Samir was dressed in a pale pair of jeans and a green jacket, he didn't want to shake hands. Sean welcomed her and shook her hand. It was wonderful to speak in the Belfast accent again for a moment, without thinking. 'We will take you to your hotel first. Two hours later, you are expected in a garage box. You will get a final training and you have to do a test, you'll see what it is all about'. They walked to a huge hall where a lot of little bars, shops and restaurants were. Siobhan looked at the people, the colours and the shops and blinked her eyes. The hall was connected to an open space, covered with a roof of glass. There were big electronic boards everywhere, with timetables for the trains. Sean explained that they would take the train to the central station of Amsterdam. Samir was standing in line at a yellow ticket machine. Sean said: 'What did you think of the desert, did you miss home?' 'I don't know, Sean, it was too hot and lonely. I missed my parents very much and my friends in Schull. I don't like to lie to no one. They don't deserve this at all. It is really strange, if you want to send a mail and have to make up all sorts of things, so they don't get suspicious. Now I will have to lie again about where I am.' 'This is the pressure we to have to deal with, this will only get worse, Siobhan. Think about your goal, at last some kind of retaliation for the ones who never got punished, for the discrimination of our people for centuries, for the killing of innocent people without any reason, and it never stopped,' Sean said. Samir had taken three tickets out of the yellow machine. He motioned they had to walk to an escalator. It was full of people who rushed downstairs to catch a train. Siobhan still had to get used to the bright colours, sounds and impressions of all that surrounded her. They entered an underground platform with pillars in the middle. For a moment she closed her eyes, she thought for a moment: 'If I could vanish into one of those pillars, just like in the movie of Harry Potter. He just went in with his suitcases and his owl on a trolley.' Suddenly her secret mission was weighing very heavy on her shoulders, she wished she could abandon it somehow. Siobhan felt very lonely because she couldn't share this part of her life with the ones she loved. A train approached the platform and the doors opened. Masses of people tried to get out, masses of people tried to get in. The train started to move in a jerky way. Its balcony was overcrowded. In the corner a young woman stood, dressed in a long black outfit and a headscarf, with a little child in a buggy. A man with a short leather jacket and a fat belly leaned against the buggy, there was not enough room on the balcony. He looked with disgust down upon the woman and her child. He said to the man next to him: 'It won't take long before they will change the laws in our country, so that our girls and women are forced to were a headscarf too, it's terrible.' The other man nodded, he said: 'Where in heaven's name will this end?' 'My daughter is working as a teacher at a secondary school in the west of Amsterdam. Every day Moroccan pupils are shouting at her for no reason. Scum of the earth, that's what they all are. 'Leaving our country, that's what they should have done, yesterday, all of them. Geert Wilders is the only politician in Holland who dares to say that out loud. What a bunch of cowards they are, the rest of the politicians in the Hague. I hope after the next elections they will all disappear for once and for all!' 'Oh well, more and more are still coming to Holland,' the other man said. The young woman turned her head away. Her child was sleeping peacefully. 'Yes, and they are breeding like rabbits, goddamn, it should be forbidden!' The train slowed down. Samir clenched his fists in his pockets. The doors opened and Samir, Sean and Siobhan stepped out of the train. Siobhan looked at the huge masses of people in the railway station. It was an immense stately hall with historical ornaments and a curved ceiling. Again she wished she could vanish into the crowd an run away from her escorts. She winked her eyes while leaving the station. 'I am escorting you to your hotel, Samir is going directly to the garage box. It's better that we are not seen together too many times.' Without saying a word Samir disappeared from the street they were walking in. It had a lot of bars, restaurants and trendy shops. Siobhan felt the liberty all around her, it was a feeling of freedom. For a moment she felt one with the people surrounding her in their different outfits. The people were white, black or they had eastern looks. 'It must be wonderful to live in this city,' she thought. Sean motioned they had to turn into to a side street. It was a narrow street with a few bars and now and then large windows surrounded by red lights. Behind the window women with hardly any clothes on were sitting, some of them were smoking. She had never seen anything like this in Ireland, women who showed their body without any shame to people who were passing by. 'This is the red light district, Amsterdam is famous for it. The Dutch are very liberal concerning sex, Siobhy,' Sean said, and he continued: 'We are almost there.' 'You want to leave me with these hookers?' 'Don't worry, it's a decent hotel, right at the corner of this street.' The hotel was situated in a narrow but high building with a stepped gable, a typical Dutch canal house. Narrow grey stairs connected the entrance of the hotel with the street. The reception was just a small desk. A black man greeted them kindly. He looked at the reservations and gave to Siobhan, now Donnah Nugent, the key of her room. Sean gave her the address where she had to be in two hours' time, and a map of Amsterdam. He gave her a kiss on the cheek and left the building. Siobhan carried her trolley to the first floor. Her room was situated next to the stairs. 'If I need to flee, I can run down the stairs directly,' she thought. She opened the door of her hotel room. The room had a high ceiling with a design lamp. A double bed which was covered by a dark red bedspread, a simple desk and long narrow table with a flat screen television filled the room. She opened the door of the bathroom. She liked its design, a huge bath next to a sink with a large mirror above it, just as the toilet all in a light yellow colour. She looked in the mirror. She still had to get used to her new outlook; her dark brown hair, glasses and her brown eyes which was the colour of the contact lenses. 'Hello Donnah Nugent,' she said to herself. She opened her trolley to get clean underwear. After her session in the garage box she would directly go to the restaurant to have dinner with David. Siobhan was curious what would happen, but she also realized he posed a risk. Actually everyone who came too close was a risk and formed a danger to her new identity. The time in Dingle and Schull when she could play music, meet friends, go out and think about which study she would like to do later, seemed in a far distant past as if it had been another life altogether. As if she had been another person with an open future. It would have been easy to leave for the United States, since Boston College offered her a scholarship. But she had chosen to study History and Anthropology at the Queens University in Belfast. The History school had an excellent department of contemporary History, specialising in English and Irish history. She had to get used to Belfast again after a lovely period in the Republic. The warm water of the bath embraced her body. For a moment she drifted away and forgot all about the present.

10.

The little building of the Anglican church of Tavira was situated near the tidal river. The wide river divided the city in two parts. The city had a pleasant atmosphere with its little stores, terraces, and a small museum about the Algarve and its history. A beautiful park was nearby, it had a lot of flowers and palm trees. The beautiful traditional Portuguese houses were covered with azulegos, tiles which formed magnificent patterns with intense colours. In the middle of the city there was a square. During the summer music festivals were held here in the open air, sometimes with the original fado. A lot of tourists came to visit Tavira. Overlooking the city was the Arabic Castle, remains of the period the Arabs had controlled Portugal and Spain. In the centre of the remains of the castle was an Arabic garden with lovely flowers, bushes and trees, the colours were wonderful, and so was the smell. Father Steve worked already for a long period as an Anglican pastor for the English community in the Algarve. A lot of the British were retired, the well-to-do had large villas and lived most of the year in this part of the world. At times people needed a service in the Algarve, for example when a loved one died. There was a gathering with friends and family before the dead body was transported back to the UK and buried over there. Father Steve helped in the whole process, he was the first contact if the family still had some sort of Christian faith. Sometimes a person just wanted to talk to him about a matter of conscience, or it could be he or she wanted to take part in one of the group meetings he organised. Father Steve was happy he could do something for his fellow Englishmen. Recently a woman had called him; it was a lady called Ann Pigden, from a park nearby the Spanish border. He knew the park, and had been there a few times to visit people. She wanted to talk with him, if it suited him. That same day he had time, so she would arrive around two o' clock in the afternoon. Actually he didn't know her in person, but of course she was welcome for a conversation. That morning he had prepared the meeting room for a group to talk about mourning. When someone died the people who were left behind always had a lot of questions: 'Why did my loved one have to die? What am I going to do all on my own? Stay here or go back to England?' They were experiencing a lot of inner confusion. But he had a hunch Ann Pigden was walking around with something else on her mind. The chairs were in a circle, the flowers on the table on a white tablecloth, the teacups on the side table. Everything was ready for this evening. He left the building. There was enough time to have an early lunch in the neighbourhood before his meeting this afternoon. Father Steve loved Tavira, he lived there for more than ten years now. Not once had he thought of going back to the county of Kent. In the Algarve he had found a way of living just like the other people from the UK, who reminded him of the times in Great Britain some fifty years ago. People still knew each other personally, they still had respect for law and order. There still was some kind of social order then. A few months ago he had experienced with deep sorrow this Great Britain had vanished forever. He had to go to Kent for a training of the church. No one greeted him in the streets. He was pushed aside and spit at by some young Muslims who were dressed in traditional robes. He had felt like a stranger in his own country, and felt relieved when he could take the plane back to Faro after a week.

He whistled a little tune and sat down at his usual table at the restaurant 'The Dolphin' overlooking the River. The staff spoke English very well, they knew exactly how to please him. He hardly had to point at the menu. Sometimes he tried to speak some words in Portuguese, it was always answered with a smile. Portuguese liked it when foreigners tried to speak their difficult language. The pronunciation, the swallowing of some of the syllables and the words that did not seem to have a link with words he knew from French or Spanish; it was all a given just like the Portuguese culture and history. Father Steve ordered a tuna salad, a glass of white wine and some bread. He looked at the river which seemed peaceful. Halfway the bridge someone played guitar, it resounded over the river. Some people stopped and threw some coins in a hat. For a moment father Steve felt a blessed man. He felt sorry for his colleagues in Kent who had to do their work in a divided society. A month ago another incident had occurred. In quiet Kent, with its lovely landscape, a group of young militant Muslims had gathered at Canterbury cathedral. They were waving large black flags and wanted to enter the cathedral, where the boys' choir was just practising. The group of Muslims was shouting : 'IS, IS, IS will come'. The boys in the cathedral were very scared, the police who arrived at the scene could prevent at the last moment that the cathedral was entered by the militants. The inhabitants of Kent were shocked, rudely disturbed in their daily rhythm. The incident was discussed intensely in the British media. A lot of commentaries were given by experts on Islam and local politicians but the result was that the people didn't feel reassured at all. On the contrary, the public had the feeling they had to be calmed down and soothed, that the real problems were not addressed in any way. Great Britain not only had a large Muslim population, but also an Indian community and a black one, too. In all sorts of educational projects the government tried to prepare young people for a place in society. This hardly worked out. Large groups were discriminated, not only on the job market. This led to frustration and sometimes groups of Muslims , the black and Indian community were fighting each other in cities like Manchester and Leeds. Those cities had a reputation for this kind of disturbances. But now the lovely, and historical Kent was hit by an act of violence and Great Britain was hit in the heart of its existence. Father Steve shuddered. He looked at his watch, it was almost time to go. He paid his bill and said goodbye to the restaurant owner. While walking towards the building of the Anglican church he saw a stocky figure with black hair standing in front of the building. 'Sorry I am late,' father Steve said. 'I had lunch at the river,' He shook hands with Ann and mentioned his name. 'Ann Pigden, a pleasure to meet you, how do you do?' 'Good. Please be welcome and follow me, I will make us a cup of tea first.'

Ann wiggled behind the vicar, and upstairs they went. She was sweating heavily, it was just too hot for her. She felt very nervous and uncertain. As if father Steve guessed her thoughts he said : 'Don't worry Ann, everything will turn out fine in the end, (and he thought I hope so…), you can trust me.' Father Steve opened the door of a little room and offered Ann a chair. He went to the kitchen and brewed a pot of tea. Together with some biscuits, milk, two porcelain teacups and a few lumps of sugar. 'How would you like your tea?' 'Only a little bit of milk, I need to watch my weight.' Indeed she had to watch her weight, she had become dangerously fat. Her doctor had warned her heart was in danger, and for sure she had also to stop smoking. She just could not quit. When she was smoking she could feel at ease for one second only. She took a sip of her tea, it was impossible now to run away from the man who was sitting opposite her, one way or another she had to talk to him. Perhaps she shouldn't have come here in the first place, why in heavens' name did Lucy push her so much? 'What can I do for you Ann?' father Steve asked. 'Actually I don't know how to start, really.' She coughed. 'I have terrible nightmares all the time, and they keep on repeating themselves.' It was silent for a few minutes. Father Steve hoped she would continue telling her story, but she didn't. He asked : 'Most of the time a repeating nightmare has a message for us, something our consciousness finds it hard to carry. What is it that you can't bear Ann?' 'I keep on dreaming again and again that a man is falling down. There is blood streaming out of his back, sometimes there is a boy, too, standing next to him. He is bending over to the man, he turns his face towards me and I see one eye is missing, blood is streaming out of the hole. I wake up sometimes screaming, or so Lucy, my partner, says. I am sweating heavily, I can't sleep anymore. I think: 'I am a murderer, I am a murderer, all the time. I will never again experience peace in my soul. This dream is God's punishment, it's all my fault, a voice in my head is telling me this. On the other hand, I know I did my duty for England, it can't all be my fault. But the voice in my head never stops.' 'Why do you think the voice is telling you this, Ann?' 'The voice is telling me that Bloody Sunday is my fault. I shot, yes, I had to shoot for it was an order and I obeyed. I could have run away and refuse to shoot, but I didn't.' 'Did you actually see that you hit someone?' 'It was all chaos, one big chaos. We were afraid of the people who came towards us. I don't remember if I hit someone or not. But I did fire some rounds of bullets, sure.' 'Ann, it is most courageous of you to tell me all this. You realize you were part of this terrible event. But it was war, don't you forget this. You can always judge events of the past in the present, but at that time you had to act in that situation, which was very difficult. I understand this is all very hard to bear for you and I can't take away your nightmares, but try to be gentle for yourself. You know they have done research on Bloody Sunday and we as the British nation apologized, let this also be your personal excuse. Many things in history happened which we would have liked to be different. Take for example the First World War, how many boys of ours were chased into death?' 'The way you say it, I used to think along the same line, but at the moment I don't know what to think anymore, what if I really did shoot somebody?' It might have been someone who was a father, an uncle or a brother. Probably I've hurt a family very badly. Their lives never could be the same after that day.' 'Don't torture yourself Ann, you can't rewrite history, try to live in the present with your partner Lucy, here in Portugal. You served our country well in a very difficult time during the troubles. You defended our values. We tried to help Northern Ireland the very best we could, and look now what mess they have made of it themselves!' 'These could have been my words, father, but I doubt everything these days. 'If it keeps on bothering you, come back to this place, see if it does you any good. Try to take some distance symbolically. Lay down some flowers for the one you think you shot. I don't say you did, but it might be a way to come to terms with everything.' 'I will think about it. Perhaps I can go there together with Lucy.' 'That's a good idea, Ann.' 'I am very tired now, I get very tired whenever I speak about the past, father.' 'Well let's wrap up this conversation now,' father Steve said. 'If you want we can make an appointment for another meeting, when would it suit you?' 'I don't know, can I call you when I feel like it?' 'Yes, of course, my door is always open for you! If you would like you always can take part in one of our groups, or you are welcome in our service on Sunday.' 'I will think about it,' Ann said and she shook hands with father Steve. She left the room and slowly heaved herself downstairs.

11.

Samir hurried home. He didn't feel obliged at all to shake hands with that Irish woman, she was not only of little importance to him but also for his organisation, called the Dawn of the True Islam. A pawn in the game, that would take care of the testing of the secret weapon: the little poison ball. She was just a footnote, someone who brought money into the organisation. Samir obeyed his parents totally on the outside. Those people had no idea what really was keeping him busy at all. They were hardworking people, originally from the Rif, the northern mountainous part of Morocco. They emigrated to the Netherlands to build a better and more prosperous future for themselves and for their children. In a way they succeeded. His father worked in a cocoa factory for a very long period now, in the Dutch city of Zaandam, close to Amsterdam. He provided the family with a reasonable income. His mother was running the household and was part of a neighbourhood group where she attended Dutch lessons. The Dutch women took care of her well, with their painted and short reddish hair. The group they were coaching consisted of Moroccan, Turkish, Somalian women and also a few from Surinam and the Dutch Antilles islands. They discussed their lives, but also that of their families, they celebrated each other's festivals sometimes, with homemade food of the original country they came from. Some of them spoke reasonably good Dutch. The sister of Samir, Ayisha was studying law at the University of Amsterdam. She had graduated from a grammar school with high scores. A few teachers convinced her parents to let her start and study at university. His brother Said studied architecture, he was an excellent student. Samir himself followed a vocational education of Social Work at the Horizonten college, a perfect cover. He tried to do his assignments on time, to get good notes on a test from time to time. His aim was to be a normal student, and not get noticed. But he was living strictly by the Islamic laws, in secret as if this was his hidden personality. He went to the mosque regularly, prayed every day. He read and recited the Koran every day, to keep his Arabic up to date. His parents celebrated the month of Ramadan. But his father wasn't interested in going to the mosque, just like his sister and brother too no interest. From time to time Samir was wearing a traditional kaftan, but not too often, as he didn't want to attract attention. The imam of the mosque he attended was an elderly, very friendly man. In no way he wanted his community to draw attention in a negative way. He was careful what he did and didn't say. He just wanted to be there for his flock. Once a local newspaper called him a typical Dutch 'Polder imam' which meant something like totally one with Dutch society. Sometimes he had a meeting with Christian and Jewish leaders. He never spoke out loud the radical texts that could upset Dutch society. The imam still felt like a guest in the Netherlands, and that was how he behaved. The weekly Friday prayer, a marriage, a funeral:

he helped his community at those events as much as he could. Sometimes parents asked him for a bit of advice; a son who wanted to marry a non-muslim girl, a girl who was not prepared to be married off. Most of the time everything was solved in a reasonable way. He never heard of young Muslims who were getting radical, in his community this could never happen, he thought. He had talked to Samir now and then, but his increasing interest in Islam was nothing special in the eyes of this Imam. Samir's education went well, he didn't bother his parents and he was a good student at learning how to recite the Koran. This young man was part of a helpful family, that was always ready to help other people.

12.

Samir had to hurry, he just had a snack at the cafeteria. He was very hungry, but he had to be in time at the garage box. Sean, his partner in crime, insisted on being present at the last briefing for the assignment of that Irish woman. Samir had rather he wouldn't be there, the less people knew about the whole operation the better. But the London terror cell of the Dawn of The True Islam had agreed, since the real IRA gave them a lot of money, one of the reasons the secret weapon could have been developed at all. The garage box was registered under the Dutch name of Hans van Straaten, who used the box to store his surfboard and other stuff. To make the cover up complete a surfboard was hanging on the wall. A tarpaulin covered some boxes. The boxes contained advanced transmitting devices. You could communicate around the world without being traced, it went beyond the normal wireless systems. Lately there had been a lot of contact with the training camp in Libya, the cells in London and Amsterdam. If that Irish woman would execute her task in the south of Portugal, she would not be operating within the untraceable wireless network. Samir took tram number 12 and got off three stops before the street of the garage box, the last part of his route he rather walked. After opening the revolving door he closed it directly. Very proud he looked at the boxes. Without a trace they could communicate all over the world in their own network, too sophisticated for the local police and secret services all around the globe. It would be almost impossible get inside 'The Dawn', because of this advanced technology that was developed in London. The very fine education that many of the members of 'The Dawn of the True Islam' had had at universities in the West, was very useful to the organisation. This technical knowhow was the basis for the development of the secret weapon; the little poison ball that could destroy all life in a certain space and disappear completely after it did its job. When it was successfully tested it could be used anywhere in the world. Samir felt very important and proud to be part of the organisation, that was going to make its name in the world. It was a world with a lot of dying states, that had no moral values anymore, especially in his own country, the Netherlands. Take his sister for example, she did not wear a headscarf, she dated an unbeliever, a Dutch man. His parents hardly ever went to the mosque. Dutch society was full of gay people who participated in the Gay pride parade, on boats in the canals, there were drunk people who walked along the streets and hookers sitting behind large windows. Luckily that strange fellow Theo van Gogh was slaughtered in a ritual way some years ago. He was the one who called his people goatfuckers. A matter of justice that this man was killed by one of his brothers. Allah is holy, this brave martyr was now in a Dutch prison, serving a long sentence. His reward would be enormous. The Dutch secret service, the AIVD, did all sorts of research after the death of this cursed infidel.

The AIVD went looking for Islamic terror cells, lone wolves and they even visited schools to check on pupils. The organisation of the Dawn of the True Islam that already existed in those days had not been discovered. There was a beep from one of the devices. Duty was calling now. Samir could see the Irish woman and that man Sean, they were approaching the garage. The women had to succeed this test; it would be a test of her reliability to 'The Goal', of her mental strength and her knowledge of the secret weapon and how to use it effectively when she was ordered to do so. If she passed she was in, if she didn't, she had a big problem and so did the organisation. She knew too much, and one way or another they would have to get rid of her.

13.

Siobhan was at a gathering of the study group she was a member of in the History Department of Queens University of Belfast. Every member had done a piece of research about Bloody Sunday. She found out in the archives of a local newspaper that a man was shot in the back in a peaceful demonstration on Bloody Sunday. The man collapsed with a little boy holding his hand. In the confusion of that situation no one really knew who this man was. The situation had been one big chaos. In the chaos peace loving demonstrators were shot in the back, chased at as if they were wild beasts, as if they were criminals. Siobhan felt a deep feeling of hatred. She thought her father had to do something with this event, but he didn't even want to talk about it. He always said : 'Book closed, period. We have to live now, let the past be the past.' One of her study mates did research on how the British government had dealt with this tragic event. For a long time the role of the British soldiers and their superiors was not investigated, nor had there been any excuses to the people of Northern Ireland. In the eyes of the British the people of Northern Ireland were guilty themselves, they had caused the troubles in the first place. Later there had been some investigations, but all from the British side. Much later, in 1998, there had been new research, the committee was named after Lord Saville of Newdigate. It took twelve years to get to a conclusion for the time being, that some soldiers could be punished, because they had shot at innocent civilians. The investigation was published on the 15th of June, 2010. David Cameron, the British prime minister, apologized. As if the wounds could be healed and the past could be forgotten and be forgiven. Siobhan knew this, but she wanted to know more. Not only what had happened to her father exactly, but also who shot who. She wanted to know it all. She left the university and took the city bus to the catholic part of Belfast. Her parents still lived there where she grew up. While thinking about her parents she swept away tears from her eyes with her hand. The bus stopped, she thanked the bus driver. Her father had opened the door already, before she could ring the doorbell. They kissed each other on the cheek. Her mother offered her a cup of tea. 'We don't see you much lately, are you okay?' she asked. 'Do you eat enough?' 'you look so skinny, did you lose weight?' 'You don't work too hard, do you?' 'No mum, don't worry about me. Our research at the university is going very well, but speaking of this, I would like to talk with you dad, about Bloody Sunday, I know that you don't like to talk about it but still.' 'Sit down, Siobhan, and drink your tea first.' 'I really want to know dad, what do you remember of that day?' 'I know you must have been a child at that time, but please tell me!' 'It's a terrible story, Siobhan, and up till now I never wanted to put a burden on your shoulders and I still don't want to do this.' 'I want to know.' 'Alright then, I will tell you what I remember. It is quite difficult for me actually, I have a dream all the time, over and over again. I want to flee , but my feet are glued to the ground. My legs won't move, not an inch. A man dressed in a green suit wants to grab me. But before he can do this another man drags me along. I hear the same shouting over and over again: 'Help me, help me.' I see an eye, which has a hole in it, with no end, it is totally endless. Suddenly a river of blood from the eye comes in my direction, so much blood that I almost drown in it. Most of the time I wake up after this image.' 'Do you often have this dream, dad?' 'Yes.' 'But what do you remember of the reality of that day itself?' 'Uh, I don't know how to start. It is the first time I speak about it openly, even your mother doesn't know a lot.' 'Try it dad, please try.' Her father sighed. He started to tell, pausing every now and then.' My father held my hand, we were walking in a large group, we didn't walk very fast at all. I heard a very loud popping sound, just like fireworks. I felt my father slowly slumped. I saw there was a lot of blood coming from his mouth. Someone must have picked me up, for the next moment I was lying behind a wall with a man. He stroked my hair. I didn't feel anything, anymore, but later I felt a heavy pain in my belly. More than that I can't remember.' 'Dad, why didn't you tell me this before?' 'Why not?' You always said to me that grandpa died early of a disease!' 'I didn't want to talk about all of this, and if you wouldn't have asked me my lips would have been sealed forever. Please Siobhan let it be, focus on your future, maybe you can teach something useful as a teacher of history, after you finished your studies. That hatred answered by hatred doesn't solve anything, it only creates more hatred and negativity. 'Excuse me?' The Orangemen create hatred every year, again and again. Lately a bomb explosion of the real IRA was prevented, as a reaction to a march of the Orangemen. They were spitting, shouting and singing throughout our neighbourhood, just to provoke us. I don't see any point dad, why we would accept this all the time, why in heavens name do they try to humiliate us all the time?' Because they think they own the truth and we are 'lower' people or so?' I think this is insane, really insane, your own father was shot!' 'I know this is terrible, but as long as we keep on thinking in 'they' and 'us' there never will be a safe future for you and my grandchildren. I try to forgive although this is very hard for me. For me that's the only way to cure from all of this.' 'Sorry dad, I can't follow you there. I don't believe in forgiving if the offender isn't punished in any way. Covered by the British government, it is so easy and cheap. Why don't you stand up for yourself?' 'Siobhan, this is not the way I want to handle this, I want some peace in my life now.' 'You want to suppress it all, that is what you mean!' The murderer of my granddad simply cannot run around free in this life, if he or she is still alive. We have judges, who can judge if this person could still be condemned. From my point of view: behind bars with this idiot.' 'My request is: please let it rest and focus on your future.' Siobhan knew it was no use to contradict her father. But she decided to find out who killed her grandfather, whom she had never known. It was her duty she thought. She put her hands in the pockets of her jeans, her fists clenched.

14.

Ann and Lucy were invited by Nelson, just like the rest of the park to attend the 'farewell service' of the Anglican church. Nelson's wife Diana had suddenly died. Despite the excellent care in the hospital in Faro, she left this life during the night. Nelson was inconsolable. He walked around not knowing what to do, with his little dog staring at him as if he was completely empty inside. Sometimes he shook his head and mumbled a few words. Everybody felt deeply sorry for him. He was invited to dinner by people, or they had a drink with him. The dead body of his wife was flown over to Great Britain directly after she died. He would follow a few days later. Only her daughters, Nelson, a few friends and close relatives would be there. In the restaurant of the park photos of Diana were displayed; Diana as a young woman, their wedding pictures, Diana with her two daughters, Nelson and Diana on a trip together in South Africa. Diana dressed in a beautiful white outfit. The table was decorated with white flowers and ribbons. Everything was well taken care of. People could write something in a big notebook. After the service Nelson had arranged food and drinks. 'A light and warm get together, I hope,' he had written on the invitation. Of course father Steve would be in charge of the ceremony. Diana often volunteered in the Anglican church in Tavira, everybody loved her, she always had a sincere interest in the people around her. She set up crowdfunding for parents who couldn't afford to buy books for their children's high school in Tavira but in Villa Real de St. Antonio as well. Since the economy in Portugal wasn't doing too good there were a lot of parents who couldn't buy books for their children. The project was much appreciated. Ann felt very nervous, because father Steve would arrive shortly, the man who knew her big secret. She felt as if everybody looked at her with different eyes in the park, the woman with a dark and hidden past, the woman who probably had killed. She felt like an inferior creature. She felt she shouldn't be in the ceremony at all, she wasn't worthy. Suddenly she had the feeling she almost choked, as if she couldn't breathe anymore. 'I am a disgusting insect. People think I am human, but I'm no more than a fat insect dressed up to make me look human. She closed her eyes. Lucy touched her hand for a second and said: 'Father Steve just arrived, say hello to him Ann.' Ann tried to get up. Her body felt so terribly heavy, she could hardly stand on her feet. Father Steve turned around and saw her effort, he immediately went round to greet her. He shook her hand and said: 'Good to see you, Ann. Good that you are part of the ceremony. There is a place on earth for you too. Please be seated.' More and more people came to the terrace of the small restaurant of the park, where the service would take place in the open air. Everybody hugged Nelson and each other. You could see this meant a lot to him. A man tapped on the microphone to test if it worked. It was okay, since everybody turned their head to the sound. He announced that

Nelson would say something first, then father Steve would take over and the last part was for anyone who wanted to say something, too. Nelson walked to the front, everybody stared at him. 'Dear people, thank you all for coming. I know Diana would have really appreciated this very much. She is still very close to me. I can hardly imagine she isn't with us anymore. Everything went by so quickly. For me it feels absurd that this cruel fate had to hit her, she who was so helpful in every way. To be honest, I don't understand anything anymore, murderers live a hundred years and my Diana had to die of a terrible disease, life just isn't fair.' Nelson couldn't say a word anymore, he was totally overwhelmed by grief. He went slowly back to his seat. Father Steve took over. He read a text from the Bible which he had chosen carefully : 'Love your neighbour as yourself'. In a short speech he said, we so often forget to love ourselves first. That means accepting ourselves as we are, also with our uncertainties, our anger, our fears. Do not suppress this, but simply let it be like it is'. In his opinion it was alright to be angry and feel deep grief when a loved one suddenly died. Share it with other people. Give it some space to be. He invited everyone who wanted to say something to do so. Ann wiggled forwards and opened her mouth. 'Dear people, I am deeply shocked that our beloved Diana had to die so soon. She deserved life more than I do. I wished I had died instead of her.' People were astonished about what she just said and looked each other in the eye. She sat down next to Lucy. Lucy whispered in her ear: 'This was totally unnecessary Ann, really. Why are you doing this to yourself?' Jeff took the microphone. 'I only want to say I feel blessed to live in such a warm community. I can't really deal with the fact Diana is not with us anymore. Dear people this can happen to anyone of us. We should be thankful that we have this wonderful life here in Portugal, together. I will miss Diana terribly.' It was completely silent for a few minutes. Nelson thanked everybody extensively for their contribution to the ceremony. Diana would have wanted that they had a drink and a bite now. Ann and Lucy tried to avoid people and to leave while people were chatting all around them. When they arrived at their chalet Ann set down on the veranda, and Lucy made a cup of tea. 'I hope the conversations with father Steve will give her inner peace,' she thought. When she stepped on the veranda with a cup of tea for Ann, she saw that she had fallen asleep. 'Lovely,' she thought: 'One moment of rest.'

15.

Her image in the mirror was staring back at her. Her dyed dark brown hair surrounded her pale face. Even in the desert her skin remained rather white. She was slim, dressed in a sexy black dress with a deep decolleté, nothing reminded of the short period she had been like a soldier. She had decided to return to the hotel first to change. The test went very well and was done in a moment. She felt satisfied that her test had an excellent result. Even Sean gave her a compliment, something he hardly ever did. Samir was in charge of the equipment and nodded when she had passed the tests. Her real task could begin soon. Finally she could take away the life of the woman who murdered her grandfather. In no way that women called Ann Pigden had any trouble to get on with her military career, nor was she ever brought to justice for it. Her father had a lifelong trauma, not really being able to feel, and she herself had never known her grandfather. Siobhan bit her tongue from pure anger. How many times she had not been humiliated by the Orangemen? But now it was her turn to strike back, to kill that woman who had become a symbol for all of this. That she had to work together with the real IRA and Islamic extremists to reach her goal, she couldn't care less. She hoped that she could successfully test the secret weapon for them all, so that they could attack the City in London later on. 'The whole City may go to hell,' she thought. She looked at herself in the mirror again and put up some more make up. She felt excited to see that sexy David again. She knew it could be dangerous, meeting him again but she couldn't resist. 'Maybe he is a phoney as well, who knows, but no, this can't be possible,' she thought. She just wanted to have a good evening out, hopefully with a happy end in bed. The phone in her room rang. 'Your taxi has arrived, madam,' a voice said. She quickly ran downstairs, she hated the lift with its narrow space. David had invited her to a trendy popular Moroccan restaurant in the centre of Amsterdam. After ten minutes the taxi arrived at the address. Siobhan thanked the taxi driver, and she gave him a tip. From this moment on she was Donnah Nugent again, the special needs teacher who lived and worked in the northern part of London. Donnah was well prepared. She had read all about the work of a special needs teacher. How for instance people were socially connected in the neighbourhood, how they interrelated. But perhaps this knowledge wasn't needed at this date. Siobhan looked at the upper part of the entrance. It was marked by Hebrew letters. 'Strange that you enter a Moroccan restaurant through a gate with Hebrew letters, strange people, the Dutch, where else on earth can you see something like this?' She was welcomed by a friendly black man wearing a dark suit. He seemed to know which table she had to go to. David was already sitting there. He got up and kissed her on the cheek, twice. Siobhan saw he was dressed very elegantly, with a light blue shirt, a red tie and jeans. 'Donnah, it is great to see you again, you look fabulous!' 'Thanks, David. You don't look bad yourself.' The black young man moved the chair backwards, Siobhan could sit down. She felt like a princess for a moment, being served like this. A waiter asked what they wanted to drink and gave them the menu. They both ordered a lager. 'Donnah, I really enjoy meeting you again. Did you see the inner city of Amsterdam yet?' The Rijksmuseum is now open again, just like the international art museum, where I was today. There is a very interesting exhibition, all of the work of Felix Nussbaum can be seen!' 'I visited the van Gogh museum today. I always wanted to see his paintings in reality, I am an admirer of his work, especially the sunflowers. I had a reproduction in my room when I was a child,' Siobhan answered. She looked at the menu and decided to take a starter with olives. 'Do you know what you would like to have, Donnah?,' David asked. 'I would like a starter with olives and the main course : 'A variation on couscous'. David wanted the same thing. He beckoned the waiter who was dressed in a colourful robe. He ordered a bottle of red wine to go with the food. Siobhan bit on her tongue; she should not forget to speak with a British accent all the time, and keep in mind not to tell personal stuff. At the same time she felt a warm glow going through her body, she had to admit David moved her one way or another. 'Don't think with your body, she said to herself, keep your head cool!' The waiter brought the bottle of wine, he knew what he had to do. He poured just enough wine, it filled the glass halfway. He gave it to David, who smelled and took a little sip, he nodded and said: 'This wine is excellent.' The waiter poured the wine in both glasses. Siobhan said: 'This wine is really good!' 'I love its taste!' She drank her wine, and David filled her glass again. She felt as if her head was floating a bit. She heard David asking about her work as special needs teacher, automatically she answered his questions. David remarked he thought she was deeply involved in her job. What if David was playing a role just as she did, then they were both faking now. She wondered why this popped up in her head. But no, he was just a businessman working in the City of London, who visited Amsterdam before he had to go back to work. Perhaps she drank too much wine in a short time, nevertheless she took another sip, and she felt relaxed. 'Cheers, David,' she said a bit too enthusiastic and hoped David didn't notice it. 'Tell me something more about yourself David, you were born and raised in the better parts of London?' 'No. I grew up in Carlisle. The landscape around the city is beautiful, the people living there are very friendly. I studied economics in London. I found a job in the City right after my studies and got stuck. 'What kind of work are you doing?' 'That is not so easy to explain. I am working for a bank and do research for them. We try to develop new financial products that are more transparent, after the crash in 2008 we have to be much more reliable for our clients.' 'Of course you do, it is a mess in bankers' land, people lost thousands of pounds because they bought strange products you wanted them to buy, they were cheated out of their money.' It struck David how sharp Donnah was expressing herself. Dinner was served. The starter came with the main course, at the same time. Siobhan wished David 'bon appetit'. After her period in the desert she had realized even more how wonderful it was to enjoy a good meal. She still hadn't lost her lousy habit of eating very quickly. The restaurant was overcrowded, a popular place obviously. An announcement was made for live music. 'Are they going to play Arabic music?' David asked as if he guessed Siobhan's thoughts, she was asking herself the same question. 'I like this music, it has a different tone system,' David said. Siobhan looked at him. How handsome he was, the charming way he moved his hands sometimes and the way he was dressed, it all looked perfect. Her meal tasted excellent. In the corner of the restaurant there was a kind of bandstand, the musicians installed their instruments, a beautiful young woman with long black hair dressed in a turquoise dress, a man in a white suit and another man dressed in jeans and a white shirt. Later another man entered the stage. She wondered which sounds the instruments would produce. Suddenly they started to play. After a minute the women started to sing. She had a wonderful warm voice. The restaurant became quiet, as if the visitors had respect for the singer, as if she had a natural authority. Siobhan enjoyed the music very much, she closed her eyes to focus on the sound. She missed to play her violin. When the first song ended everybody clapped their hands. The singer made a dashing bow towards the public. 'Do you like this kind of music, Donnah?' I saw you enjoyed it.' Siobhan couldn't say anything for a moment, she felt her cheeks started to glow. David came close and he gave her a kiss on her mouth. As an answer she put her hand on one of David's. She took another sip of her wine, the glow in her body became even stronger. 'I don't feel like eating any more, do you?' David asked. 'No, me neither.' 'I'll pay, your place or mine?' 'Your place,'

Siobhan answered. David paid the bill. While walking outside David looked back over his shoulder and observed the big Hebrew letters written above the entrance of the restaurant. He grabbed Siobhan and kissed her intensely. A taxi stopped. After ten minutes they arrived at a high narrow building, which was situated near a bridge over a canal. Siobhan looked at the lights of the lanterns that were shining into the dark water of the canal. The little waves of the water of the canal made the mirror of the lights move gently. A porter, who stood in front of the hotel which had five stars on its outer wall, opened the door for them. He wore a high classical hat and a long black coat. 'It is as if I am entering Disney World,' Siobhan thought. She felt surprised that she was seeing all sorts of details, while her body was on fire, longing for David. They passed a huge hallway, with a marble floor and large paintings hanging on the wall in baroque style. In the corner there were palm trees in large pots, in the middle you could see a small fountain with water splashing. It gave the hall a special atmosphere. The elevator seemed to be made of pure gold from the outside. 'Well if I would like to make love in my artificial reality, this is the perfect spot,' Siobhan thought. The door of the elevator opened. As soon as it closed its door David started to kiss her and grabbed her breasts. She stroked his hair with one hand, while the other hand went slowly down his body and stopped at his male organ. The lift stopped at the fourth floor. David guided her towards his room, which actually was a suite, with classical furniture in the Jugendstil style. A huge painting was on the wall, showing a hunting scene with horses and hounds. 'Donnah,' David whispered, 'you are so beautiful!' He carefully unzipped her dress, she unzipped his trousers. They fell down on the king size bed. 'Donnah, Donnah', David whispered while he was ejaculating. A moment Siobhan let go of all her thoughts while she shouted when her orgasm let her body glow from head to toe. Her mind was very clear again, directly after this moment. 'How do I get rid of him, without giving too much personal details?' As if he guessed what she was thinking he said: 'Donnah, I would like to meet you again, in London perhaps?' 'David, please give me your card. I will contact you when I am ready. Please don't ask me any further questions.' David picked up his trousers and gave her one of his cards, without saying anything. Siobhan rushed into her clothes, ran downstairs, and asked the porter to call a taxi for her.

16.

Samir was surprised by the excellent test results of that Irish women. She was smart, this had been obvious during her stay in the desert, in the training camp. In a very short time she learned how to handle the secret weapon, the little poison ball in different situations. Also, she had learned in no time how to use the intricate communication system. Her body was well trained and extremely fit now. She was not only the perfect candidate to test the secret weapon, she had become a liability to his organisation, 'the Dawn of the True Islam'. With so much inside knowledge she could pose a threat, if she and her organisation, the real IRA, decided to leave the operation. He had to consult with the cell in London, perhaps it was better to get rid of her after a successful test in such a way that it looked like she died a natural death. But this also could be very dangerous of course, the police could start an investigation, the real IRA would for sure start asking questions and this probably would not be the only action from their side. One way or another this woman could cause problems. But first she would have to get out of Portugal without being noticed after she had completed her assignment. He looked at his watch, it was late, he had no time to contact London, he had to go home and do his homework for the college where he studied social science. He hated the subject 'Society communication', which he had to prepare for tomorrow a soft bullshit assignment about nothing. But even more so he hated the teacher who taught it. A stupid woman with short red hair, who dressed herself in short but colourful strange outfits. When she was bending over you could see directly into her t-shirt and see her white boobs. But it was even worse when this woman opened up her mouth. She spoke about respect for each other's culture, about getting a better position in the Dutch society than your parents had in their days, about your behaviour in your future job, about writing a correct letter of application. But the most irritating about her was, that she insisted to have 'confidential conversations' with him. Again and again she offered help to Samir. She asked him all the time if he was treated well by his parents, if he felt alright, if he felt discriminated in any way.' Samir felt like an inferior monkey on show, when she asked him a personal question in public among his fellow classmates. A monkey who supposedly needed the attention of this teacher so very badly. This terrible woman, her name was Jet Kramer, really thought she and his other coach needed to talk with him after he was turned down twice for an internship. In this woman's opinion Samir was discriminated. She started to call different organisations to make very clear one of her students was discriminated, she was the only person who really cared about his fate in her opinion. Samir hated her interference, he felt ashamed, not only in front of his classmates, but also for his family. Many times when he came home from school he heard from his parents she had called again. He knew he couldn't do much about it. He had no choice. The better he did his work for school, the less his teachers and coaches had a reason to interfere. He did not wish to be watched over at all. When he did his assignments on time, when he would get sufficient notes, when he would regularly attend class, the less he would be a 'special case', or so he hoped. When Kramer wanted another 'confidential conversation' with him, he tried to behave as neutral as he could. He was told she succeeded this time to arrange an internship for him, somewhere in an intercultural elderly home. Dutch and older people of foreign origin from countries such as Indonesia, Somalia, Morocco, Turkey and the Dutch Antilles lived there together. He acted as if he was very enthusiastic about this fantastic opportunity. According to Kramer, Samir could contribute to an intercultural platform, in which elderly people could meet each other's cultures, the Dutch government hoped that the result would be a mutual understanding between the representatives of different cultures. In Samir's view this was total nonsense, since there never could be any understanding of each other's culture. But he said to Kramer that this was the chance of his life, and a big challenge at the same time. He was sure to make it a success. He hoped she wouldn't interfere anymore, since he felt already very ashamed again, when she called with the elderly home to praise him and told them that he was so talented and perfect for the job. To him this felt like she had to compensate something, as if he were someone with no intelligence, no responsibility, a poor guy who needed her recommendation. During the night, while laying in his bed, he fantasized he had a big sword to cut off her head, so that she finally shut up and couldn't call any one anymore and talk nonsense about him. Once he had a nightmare. In it, Jet Kramer opened her mouth after he cut off her head. She said: 'I'm afraid I will have to call you parents about this incident, Samir.' He woke up and panicked totally, realizing he had an erection. With great anger he looked at the assignment which had to be presented the next day. He had to create a game, in which the elderly people were going to experience each other's culture in the elderly home, but this was not all, the most awful thing was he had to motivate again and again why he chose this particular approach. He hated this even more than the game itself. Kramer had asked him if he understood he would get a note for this assignment, which was a very important part of his studies. He almost had to throw up. With pleasure he would say during the presentation : 'The whole assignment is not only total nonsense, but criminal as well. How on earth can you force old and vulnerable people to meet with each other's strange culture? Leave them alone and search another project if you want to collect your grant. You are trying to poison our elderly people so that they can't understand the True Islam anymore. I hope you understand you will get the death penalty for this.'

Of course he could never say this now, nor write it down. But in the near future when the Netherlands had become a True Islamic State, everybody would have to listen to HIM.

For now he started to write:

"I am so well motivated to make this meeting between elderly people with different cultures a huge success. It is of essential importance that we should live in an open and tolerant society, and learn the good things from each other's culture, especially older people who in their own ways can contribute to this ideal."

He surprised himself how easy he could write down this total rubbish. If he would be able to give a successful presentation, his cover up would be safe again for the coming period, no doubt about it.

17.

'You don't need to hurt yourself, Ann, it was totally unnecessary what you did during the service for Diana,' Father Steve remarked. 'And unjustly as well,' he added. 'It is time your forgive yourself. You don't even know what you did exactly.' 'But father Steve, I cannot stop my nightmares!' 'Even if I try it drives me nuts!' 'I suggest you do a form of therapy, for instance hypnotherapy. It is a way to let go of controlling everything in life, and to get closer to your subconscious. Or a posttraumatic stress handling course of some sort.' 'How and where ?', Ann asked, 'You know my Portuguese is very poor, it's no use at all.' 'Yes, I do. But I also know a spiritual centre in Porto. It is a centre for spiritual healing, it's English spoken. A yogi from India is the leading man.' 'From India?' 'What on earth am I going to do with a wog from our former colony, India?' 'That mister, guru or whatever he may be is not waiting for me, at least that is what I think. And what does this mean: 'spiritual healing'? I thought you were ordained, a vicar of the Anglican church!' 'Of course I am, but sometimes you need to see everything in a wider perspective outside your own little church square, Ann.' I've met the yogi once at a conference of different religions in Lisbon. He is a very inspiring, humane and open-minded man. I am serious about this,

Ann, maybe the workshops and healing sessions of the centre can give you a bit of inner peace. I'll give you their brochure.' 'But father, how on earth can I keep this a secret I do not want the residents of the park to know about this at all. You know just as well as I do, they will start to gossip about this right away. They will think that I have become totally nuts! There is a group that talks about me already.' 'Listen to me, Ann, what is more important now: is it your own inner healing or what people might say about you?' 'You can tell people of the park you are going on a city trip with Lucy or so, my lips will be sealed.' Ann looked at the brochure with distaste. A photo of a sort of eastern castle with all kinds of different towers was used as a logo on the front page. She opened the brochure, all sorts of different treatments were offered, workshops and therapy with a physical and psychological dimension. One attracted her attention, a workshops where you could get in touch with any suppressed emotion you had, simply by moving and singing in one tone, to become one again with your emotions and your whole being in the present. Maybe she had to follow the advice of father Steve and attend such workshops. Perhaps she could get rid of her nightmares forever, perhaps she would be able to sleep normally again. 'I don't know what to expect father, but I'll take this information with me, and I will talk about it all with Lucy. Perhaps this is an option for me. 'I am glad you will consider this possibility Ann.' 'Do I have a choice?,' Ann said, 'I won't survive another year with so many sleepless nights. Lucy says I am a prisoner of myself and the past, although we are living for years in Portugal, this has never changed. 'Like I said before, try to live in the present now with Lucy. You can't rewrite the past; no one can, it is like it is. But you can try to neutralize its content from the present. Look at it this way: it will be as if you become a spectator of your own story, without a judgement of the facts from your past. 'People acted like they acted, since it was not possible to do it in any other way, simply because of the circumstances.' 'With all due respect father, if this is true every Nazi in a concentration camp, every hangman, every war criminal could say the same thing; 'I couldn't have behaved in another way because of the circumstances. I could have left the whole scene, but I didn't do it, because I thought I had to do my duty.' 'Ann, I don't have all answers either. I only am saying try to look at the past in its perspective. Maybe this treatment in the spiritual centre in Porto can help you with this.'

Ann shook hands with father Steve. She left the building of the Anglican church in Tavira. She wanted to buy groceries at the supermarket near the railway station, to cook something special for Lucy. Maybe it would be a good idea to invite Nelson for dinner, she would ask Lucy.

18.

'You need to come to the Royal Mail building in Belfast. I will stand in front of the building. You can recognize me by the dark glasses and the black coat. How can I recognize you?' 'By my grey coat and green hat. When do you expect me?' 'At two o'clock this afternoon exactly.' The telephone connection was broken off, the less contact by phone the better. Siobhan knew it since she had contact with the real IRA. It hadn't been easy to prove she was very serious about becoming part of this organisation. She had to do tests, her background, education and current lifestyle was thoroughly screened and examined. She was questioned about her motives, why she wanted to join the real IRA at all. In the end her membership was approved. But again and again she was told that personal revenge was no motive for an attack by the real IRA. The actions were well prepared, a personal vendetta could become an obsession. The emotions involved could lead to overreacting and endangering the whole operation. Via the real IRA Siobhan found out who had killed her grandfather, and where this person was living in these days. It was quite remarkable that the organisation had asked her to test a new secret weapon which would kill this person for sure, since personal revenge was not allowed to be the main reason for carrying out an attack. But everybody could notice her intelligence, and her capability to use new information and incorporate

it into action very quickly. Besides, her alibi as a teacher in a disadvantaged area in Belfast was perfect in the eyes of the organisation. However, Siobhan asked herself how her pupils and parents would react on her sudden disappearance, but perhaps this was already worked out and she didn't need to worry at all. She looked at her watch, it was time to go. She entered bus number 64, direction centre of Belfast. It was a bleak day, it rained a lot and there was a strong wind blowing through the streets. A grey sky was over the city, the pale light down on the red bricks of the small houses, shops and government buildings, from which the Union Jack was blowing in the wind. Sometimes a sidewall of a row of houses was decorated by a wall painting. One showed two schoolchildren shaking hands with a text: "no more violence, let our children live in peace." Another mural suggested the strength of the Ulster Boys, a big man carrying long rifles and the British flag. With a large intimidating text : "We will defend our rights at all costs". Siobhan hated this image with all of her being. Not only by the Orangemen she was so often humiliated, but also by these so called 'Ulster Boys'. No police officer ever arrested one of these 'Boys'. But now the time had come to get even, one way or another the bill had to be paid by them. She was convinced this would work out according to her plan. She stepped out of the bus and walked in the direction which she knew was right. Suddenly a huge building was rising from the fog. On the roof big red letters made up the words : Royal Mail. As if it wanted to say to you : We never will leave from here, because we are Royal, and if you can't understand this you are a barbarian, an outcast or a terrorist. She turned around and saw a young man standing in front of her wearing dark glasses and a black coat. He looked at her. 'I take it you know who I am?' 'Yes Sean, of course.' 'We are going to Charlie's pub, it is near the Ramada Hotel. They walked behind each other to the pub. It was already filled with people, although it was early in the afternoon. Sean ordered two pints. The pub had only a few lights which spread scarcely any light, with the dark furniture it had a gloomy atmosphere. Sean and Siobhan took a seat in the corner near a window. 'Let us do as if we're a couple in love,' Sean said. Without any warning he kissed her. She didn't know if she liked this or not, but for sure she felt surprised. She took a gulp from her pint. 'I won't tell you fairy tales in here. This is a very dangerous mission, but for us it is of great importance. You are already screened. We know of course your background and all the details. But we think you are not only very intelligent, but also -how can I say this-, motivated to destroy the target. We think you can control your emotions very well, as well as execute this mission in a professional way. You are first going to Libya. We have set up a training camp with the international Islamic terror organisation called The Dawn of the True Islam. They developed a secret weapon, which can destroy specific targets. Afterwards it vanishes completely and it can't be traced anymore. I know this sounds a bit strange, but this technology is a reality. All information I give you is classified as 'total secret'. You may never speak about this, not even within the real IRA or the Dawn, when you don't have permission from high up. It isn't written down somewhere and we don't communicate through the normal communication systems, we have our own system. You are going to test this weapon on the murderer of your grandfather. You are trained in Libya by the Dawn of the True Islam. After a successful test there are also going to be attacks on financial centres all over the world, also in the City of London, which is important for us of course. Don't ask any questions, just do your job. You are going to Portugal as a tourist. Your target is living in a park in the eastern Algarve. When your target is hit successfully, you will quietly leave the park as a tourist. The secret weapon can't be traced as I said before, but we also want to test if a person, without being noticed, can leave the country again. The special technology of the secret weapon could be developed because some of the members of the Dawn of True Islam studied at excellent technical Universities in Europe and the USA. When you are finished with your training, you travel through Jordan and Israel to Amsterdam. This detour is not only planned to see if you are noticed by any customs officer, but also to confuse people about where you are staying. Everything I say to you, you should never forget!' 'You will get a false identity and a fake British passport. Next week we meet, at the same place and same time, in this pub. You will get your necessary papers and further instructions. 'Before you are going Sean, how in heaven's name can I leave the school where I am working?' 'This is almost impossible, everyone will start asking questions, especially my students!' 'You know you have the right to take a study leave for three months. In your name a request was already made and it was approved by the principal.' 'But how did you all arrange this?' Siobhan asked surprised. 'Don't ask me, the less you know the better it is.' Your leave will start at the end of next week. The school took measures already for a replacement. Today the official papers of approval for your study leave will be on your doormat. Say goodbye to your students the coming week in an appropriate manner, the more normal its seems the better it is.' He kissed Siobhan on her mouth, his hand stroked through her hair, she liked his gestures. He stood up and left the pub without looking back.

19.

'This is an example of how an excellent presentation should be,' Kramer said. 'Samir my compliments, you did an excellent job. Not only did you succeed in the very useful suggestions about how people can meet each other's culture, but it was also the way you presented the meeting and the game for the elderly people itself. Your note will be good or excellent. Are there any questions?' 'Yes Jet,' another student said. Her clothing was totally in gothic style, but not only that, she had piercings in her nose, black make up around her eyes and dyed black hair. 'Oh no, not that terrible woman again, can't that dragon wear a normal dress?' 'When I would be in control I would know exactly how to deal with her sort. That dragon woman's head would be shaven, a headscarf on top, fifteen lashes and a long dress, down to her ankles. If she protests, even more mandatory Koran lessons. And never name the teacher by her first name, period. 'What would you like to share with us, Julie,' Kramer said. 'I don't understand Samir why you didn't suggest to cook together and celebrate the sugar feast with the whole elderly home.' 'That's a very important question, Julie, what can you do with this precious suggestion Samir?' Samir bit his tongue and thought of an appropriate multicultural and politically correct answer. He said: 'Actually I don't know, but I will add this to my 'meeting game' and use it during my internship.' 'Very good Samir, and my compliments that you speak Dutch without an accent, and this with your background….' Samir felt very angry inside, but he said: 'Thank you, miss Kramer.' She turned to him and said: 'It is Jet, Samir, for you too,' she said with a smile. 'Dismissed, all of you, you must use the rest of the afternoon to do your homework and work on your assignments at the 'work floor'. The students left the classroom. Samir sat behind his computer like everyone in the 'work floor' room. He felt satisfied, his mission was completed with success; a good rating for his assignment and he had given everyone an answer they wanted to hear. His cover up transformed more and more into a steady role. What more could he ask for? The coming evening he had very important things to do, contact the cell of the 'Dawn' in London. He started up his computer. He had to work on his log and mail it to his coach, he filled out his log very carefully and added a friendly note.

'Dear Mr. Van Balen,
As you can see this is my log, I just worked on it. I hope you are satisfied with it! If you have any questions please don't hesitate to mail or call me.'
Sincerely yours,
Samir El Charabi.

He shut down his computer, there were hardly any teachers left who could check if you stayed until five o'clock anyway. Most students left long before that time. While he picked his jacket from the coat rack, someone was tapping him on his shoulder. 'Let me take guess,' he thought, that woman Kramer again.' It was Mr. van Balen. 'Samir, Mrs. Kamer and myself would like to have another coaching meeting with you. You have an internship now, and your presentation was good this morning, but we would like to have another chat with you. I see you wanted to leave already? You know that you need to work on the floor until five o'clock. Why did you want to quit working?' 'But Mr. van Balen, everybody is leaving early around here!'. 'No one is paying us any attention on the floor any way,' Samir thought: oops, I better could have held my tongue instead of open my mouth. For sure Mr. Van Balen and Mrs. Kramer will start talking again about my 'working attitude'. 'Are you going to leave earlier at the elderly home as well, and later in your future job?' 'You know Samir, ten others are waiting to take your place! You need to work a little harder with such a name like you have, you know this, don't you!' 'But Mrs. Kramer says I am discriminated against, and that it's forbidden by law!' 'Oh well, Mrs. Kramer is really doing her very best for you, you should be very thankful. But if you behave like this, she can't help if they dismiss you from your internship. Walk with me, young man.' Samir clenched his fists in his pocket. Van Balen said: 'Samir, no fists in your pocket, this makes a very bad impression on other people, do you have enough neat clothes for your period in the elderly home?' 'But mister van Balen why don't you ask the same question to Julie or Peter?' 'She is even dressed worse than he is!' Van Balen answered: 'It is better if you are dressed the best way you can, it is better for the name of our College.' 'What an arrogant bastard, wait after our attacks, you will squeak differently, you wally,' Samir thought. Van Balen opened the door of a small room. Three chairs stood around a grey table, a single lamp was shining from a grey ceiling. It all gave an impression as if you were in a interrogation room. 'Sit down Samir, I'll get Mrs. Kramer. 'I have to calm down, otherwise I will endanger our whole operation, this is too much credit for that terrible woman Kramer and this bastard van Balen,' he thought. 'Ah Samir it's good we can have a conversation with you,' Kramer said while entering the room. 'Your presentation was good, but we hope you realize that you are going to work with vulnerable elderly people. Of course it is positive that you can speak Arabic with some of them, this can give them a feeling of being at home, but you must also know that some of the other elderly people can have -how shall I say this- prejudice against a young lad with a lightly coloured skin, black hair and an exotic name. We have to be absolutely sure you won't get mad when people behave in offensive ways. Sometimes old people can do this, you know.' 'We want to have a chat with you every Tuesday at 5 PM in this office, is this clear to you?' 'We already contacted the elderly home about this, they totally agreed we will give you some extra coaching, we all don't want the situation getting out of hand of course.' "Thank you, Mrs. Kramer that the school is giving me this great opportunity,' Samir said softly. 'This is the most suitable answer I can give,' Samir thought. Kramer bend towards him. 'It is Jet, Samir my first name for you too,' she said with an artificial smile. 'Thank you Jet, and Mr. Van Balen, too.' He knew that Van Balen didn't like to be called by his first name at all. 'You may leave now,' Van Balen said. Samir slammed the door. Van

Balen shook his head and said: 'Jet, you mustn't be too friendly to Samir Charabi, in this case it's better to keep more of a distance. 'What do you mean by this, Herman?' 'I mean because of his islamic background, you should be Mrs. Kramer for him, and not just 'Jet'. Actually I think that is better for all of our students, we are not their friends but their teachers. Van Balen resolutely picked up his briefcase and left the room without another word.

20.

'Boa tarde, good afternoon, good afternoon.' A friendly stewardess smiled at her while she dragged her trolley into the aircraft. She checked Siobhan's boarding pass and her passport. Donnah Nugent it said below the photo. She was Donnah now, with her dark brown modern styled hair, her cherry red lips and dark eyes behind her tinted glasses. She took her seat by the window. She only had a small handbag with her, her suitcase was checked in before. Ten kilo's with summer clothes, some books, open shoes, shorts and in her toilet bag not only toothpaste, but also a small hard ball. When she had picked up her suitcase from the treadmill her first step of her mission had succeeded. No one had noticed the little poison ball in that case. After her intense weekend in Amsterdam she felt tired. The difficult test and the night with David had exhausted her. She didn't know if she ever would see him again. She couldn't deny that he was very attractive, humorous, intelligent and charming. The aircraft taxied to start the take off. Low hanging clouds seemed to push the plane down on the ground. However, the airplane took off easily, it only took a minute. No one sat down in the seat next to her, there were only a few dozen people on board. Probably there was no time for short holyday breaks anymore. Through a hole in the clouds she could see the coastline of the Netherlands beneath, slowly gliding away. She wouldn't see clouds anymore the coming period, Portugal was famous for its clear blue skies. She was curious about this country, the population, the landscape and strangely enough about the murderer of her grandfather. 'Finally justice for that bitch, if a system of law didn't work in some cases, you needed to take the law in your own hands, there wasn't any other choice,' she thought. 'A murderer cannot walk around and go unpunished, it is as simple as that. Also in the next generations lives were destroyed, her father never could talk about his feelings, had to run around with a secret and he never was able to free himself from the chains. Blocked as he was, with just a simple job. But what bothered her the most was, that he had never connected with her emotionally. That woman, that bitch; the murderer was totally protected by the British occupiers. She was never brought to trial, it was her holy mission now, to even the rotten past with this one poison ball. Although her father had begged her to leave the past alone, and to focus on her future. He thought she was on her way to make a study journey to Italy, as approved by her school ; that she was going to do research about the Renaissance in Italy, its magnificent art treasures, the structure of the city states and the independent role of civilians, breaking loose from the power and authority of the catholic church. From time to time she would mail a photoshopped picture with a little report to her school. Her laptop was configured in such a way that they could not see where she really was. No one would be able to get the IP address from which she was mailing. She looked through the little window of the plane. You could see mountains, they were covered with snow. Sometimes clouds were circling below the top, it was a beautiful sight. 'If the aircraft is crashing now, no one will survive. Some parts of the bodies can be found perhaps, a leg or an arm, remnants of bones, some clothes, a broken suitcase. We are so small in comparison to the forces of nature,' Siobhan thought. She closed her eyes, it was pleasant to have some rest before the she had to act her part again.

21.

After Samir slammed the door with a bang, he ran quickly to the corridor. He wanted to leave the building as soon as possible. He was late for his meeting in the secret communication system with the cells of London and New York, thanks to arrogant Van Balen and stupid redhead Kramer, he hated that woman even more. What on earth did those idiots think, that he had nothing else to do but listen to their stupid blabbering? Once they would have to realize that their vision of 'the multicultural society' was not only utterly stupid, but dangerous as well. As soon as the greater Islamic State would have been established, their heads were in danger. They would have to pay for the fact they treated him as a monkey with no IQ at all. In the near future he had to follow Koran lessons. Kramer would be forced to wear a niqaab. Her indecent clothing, the skirts that were too short by far, the fishnet stockings, the push up bras, it all should be burned in public together with other clothes of women who wore the same flimsy rubbish. This would teach them to keep their big mouth and behave humbly and obediently, just like his mother did. He grabbed his bicycle, with high speed he entered the street, a car hardly could avoid him and hooted loudly. After racing for ten minutes, passing three red lights, he threw his bike on the ground. As soon as he was inside the garage box he removed the surfboard gear and started the transmitting device. He saw that London, like New York, were online already. 'Allahu Akbar.' 'Allah Akbar,' the answer was from London and New York in an instant. Samir knew his vision was most appreciated by his brothers in New York and London. He felt taken seriously in contrast to his position in the Dutch society. 'Speak up, brother.' 'X is on its way to the target. If mission is completed I suggest to terminate X. X knows too much and can endanger our operations. Speak with your cell all of you, please. When X is in the country again, direct and coordinated action in all cells. 'Are you ready, my brothers?' 'Yes, we are, Salaam.' Even through their advanced communication system, which hardly could be traced, they were extremely careful in exchanging information , or to name people or locations. They assumed the secret services had developed just as the 'Dawn of the Treu Islam', and might be on their tracks. The operation had to succeed, the West that still acted as if they were superior, would soon be nothing but a footnote, hardly a trace of it would be left on the world. The terror attack on the Twin Towers would be nothing but a child's play in comparison to the actions of the 'Dawn' that were soon to come. 'Allah is the greatest, brothers, over and out.' Samir grabbed his prayer rug. While praying he raised his hands, as if he wanted to be blessed, he begged God for guidance and help. He bent over a few times and touched his sparse beard. He was afraid to wear a kaftan, he did not want to be noticed, especially not by his parents, who had no idea what he was up to. For sure his sister who studied at the university would start asking questions, she didn't want to have anything to do with this retarded hassle as she called it. She considered herself a modern Western woman. She was wearing fancy clothes, had a lot of Dutch friends and went to trendy bars and disco's. She drank wine quite often. Her study results were excellent and she prepared for a future life as a lawyer. Her lecturers gave her a lot of compliments, and they saw in her an example for other women with an exotic background. She had a Dutch boyfriend, Johan. He was studying at the university, too. Aysia and Johan had plans to live together in an apartment in Amsterdam. Samir thought that his parents were to blame for this situation. They weren't true Muslims anymore, maybe they had never been. They had adapted too much to the secularised Dutch society. His parents were too much influenced by teachers, and social workers. They were from the caste of Dutch Moroccan leftist politicians and civil servants. Samir was thinking a lot about it all, he knew he should loathe Kramer, arrogant van Balen and his parents. They were all traitors. When the True Islam ruled the World this nightmare would be over soon. His sister would have to wear a full niqaab and walk one metre behind her Muslim husband. Johan, her financee, who thought he could touch a Muslim woman without being punished, would be locked up for the rest of his life, no doubt about this. Samir smiled, only his brothers in the True Islam, that Irish bitch, who was just a pawn that served them, and her friend Sean knew what he was up to. He folded his prayer-rug, put the surfboard gear on top of the transmitting device and left the garage box. With full speed he biked home to put on his mask again. For the higher goal he was prepared to play his role of excellent college student, for the time being. His parents let themselves be humiliated by Dutch society all the time, but soon they would be liberated from their burden when the time of the True Islam arrived. Of course they would be very thankful to him that he liberated them from their prison, so that they finally could shine in the light of the True Islam. Their lives would be one big feast, their heads no longer poisoned by ideas from the pestiferous Western society. Their son was the saviour, a true disciple. Before him the shabby flat appeared from the mist. More than this Dutch society had never offered them, after long years of hard work in a factory, these arrogant politicians, teachers and social workers who were always interfering in the wrong way. Yes, he had thought about this all very well indeed. The world would totally change and he was an important part of this transition. A new Islamic Empire was arising and the World had no choice but to accept this and capitulate.

22.

The brochure of the spiritual centre of the yogi was in her bag. Ann for sure didn't want anyone to see that she had this information with her. In the park everyone would think she had gone completely nuts. It was very hot; Ann regretted that she took the train and had not asked Lucy to pick her up in Tavira by car. In front of the train station there were two statues made of bronze. A woman who waved at a soldier, who was going to do his duty for his country, far away in Africa. Every time Ann walked by she thought they were real people for a second. She entered the platform to wait for the train. There it was, the usual scene of tourists wearing hardly any clothes; shorts with most of the time a sweater that was too small, sandals or a short skirt. You heard all sorts of languages; Dutch, English, French, Scandinavian and German. Ann heard a family who spoke English with a Scottish accent. They seemed to be very happy with each other and were cheerfully chatting. Probably they could live their lives without worrying at all. She felt jealous. Together with Lucy she had tried to adopt a child from China. This never worked out, they were not married and they were gay. The usual information blared from the speakers, telling the travellers from which platform the train to Vila Real de St. Antonio would leave. The old diesel train slowly approached the train station. A young woman carried a buggy with her child out of the train on her own. She nodded no to a man who tried to help her. Ann sat down near a window. A man waved a red flag, the sign that the track was free now, and the train was about to leave. Ann looked outside at the landscape which was so familiar to her; the huge cacti, blooming oleander bushes, magnificent old olive trees and the orchards full of orange trees. For a moment she could feel inner peace, she fell asleep. She woke up when the train moaned and made a sudden movement. She shivered, the sound went completely through her body. It felt very uncomfortable, she was glad to leave the train at the next station. Its familiar silhouette approached. Lucy stood on the platform waiting for her, good old reliable Lucy, where would she be without her? The person with whom she already had gone through so many things. Lucy kissed her on the cheek. 'Let's go home, I just made a nice salad', she said. Lucy started the car, the road to the park was narrow and had a lot of holes in it. No one drove very fast around here. The landscape showed signs of drought, the colour was mainly yellow, except for the patches with palm trees. The gardens of the park had to be sprayed now every day, morning and evening. 'Nelson told me that a new guest will arrive in the park today,' Lucy said. 'It seems she is going to stay fourteen days, she rented the chalet of Rose. 'He heard from Hugo of the reception that she is from London.' 'Then she is one of us, thank God. I don't like these Dutch at all, they always have a big mouth and they know everything better, it's just terrible. Especially that blonde woman, what was her name again? Not to mention that godawful language of theirs and them buying our chalets for peanuts!' 'It's not fair, Lucy!' 'Life isn't fair, it's as simple as that.' 'Father Steve gave me information about a spiritual centre in the North, in Porto. A yogi from India is giving all sorts of therapies over there, workshops and healings too. At first I thought father Steve had gone crazy even suggesting this, but I gave it a second thought afterward. I think it might not be that bad after all. I am considering going there for a treatment. I hope you can understand this.' 'Why not?, if this helps you to live a more normal life.' 'I am glad you have these meetings with father Steve, it's a beginning and it shows you don't push away the past anymore. That something is the matter with you .' 'I love you, Lucy. You still are my partner, that is God's miracle.' 'I love you too, that is why I am sitting next to you.' The car stood in front of the gate of the park. Lucy held a little plastic card close to a little yellow pole. It gave a beeping sound, and they could pass the gate. Hugo waved through the window of the reception. In general the residents of the park felt grateful for the protection they thought they got from the people working in the reception, the men who worked in the gardens, and the man who picked up the garbage every day. But maybe this was only psychological, because the fence consisted only of barbed wire, and it wasn't high by any standard. Anybody who really wanted to do so could enter the park without any problem. The permanent British residents felt very different from the Portuguese society which surrounded them. Sometimes they had the illusion they could help the Portuguese forward, with their charity projects just like they had tried to do in the former colonies. Everything was collected for this goal: clothes for the poor children, food for the poor, stray cats and dogs, and even donkeys. In this way the English had the feeling they were essential in developing another nation. Of course Ann and Lucy not only donated money, but they helped with charity markets as well. 'Let us drink a glass of wine on the terrace,' Ann proposed. 'Okay, I'll park the car near the chalet first, you go ahead, I'll join you in a minute.' With great effort Ann managed to get out of the car. She could hardly stand on her feet because of the heat. 'Hi Ann,' Debbie said. She was standing in front of the little shop that was near the restaurant. 'Do you need something? I have new chocolate bars, they are delicious!' 'No, thanks, I don't need anything now, I'll come by tomorrow to buy some bread, thank you.' 'It's really hot today,' 'Oh Debbie, it is too hot for me.' With her hand she wiped the sweat from her forehead. With the other hand she moved the curtain which gave access to the restaurant. She walked to the terrace and sat down. There was a new waiter, a young Portuguese man. In poor English he asked what she wanted to drink and if she wanted have something to eat. She ordered two white wine. She looked at the people in the swimming pool. It was next to the terrace. Children played with their ball, the elderly people were swimming and doing their exercises in the water. You heard all sorts of languages ; Dutch, English, German, French, Portuguese and Spanish. She turned her head to the entrance of the restaurant. Her mouth fell open, she was amazed. A beautiful young woman with dark brown hair and an elegant black dress walked graciously through the opening and sat down. The new Portuguese waiter came and served her at once. Ann heard she had a beautiful voice with a British accent. She could hardly breathe anymore. She felt a warm glow going through the lower parts of her body, a feeling which she had lost already years ago. Her love life with Lucy had died a long time ago. Sometimes they held hands. Sometimes they were laying in bed next to one another, and kissed each other quickly. Lucy and Ann felt close to each other, but they didn't have sex for a very long period, it wasn't essential for them anymore. Ann was surprised that she was still able to feel arousal like this. That her body could still give her this pleasant feeling. But she assumed this beautiful young woman would not take any interest in her at all. Her body was saggy, her head full of wrinkles, containing a deeply worried soul. But she was deeply surprised when the woman walked towards her. 'Hi, I am Donnah Nugent,' she said. She put out her slim hand, it had a shining ring. 'Ann Pigden, welcome to the park.' 'Thank you. Can I ask you a question?' 'Yes, of course!' 'Do you know how far the sea is from here?' I can see the shore at a distance, but I have no idea how far it is, I don't have a car, you see.' 'It's about four miles from here. The best beach is near Manta Rota. If you don't have a car, you can rent a bike. Most tourists do this when they only stay for a couple of weeks. I heard you rented the chalet of Rose?' 'It's a beautiful chalet, but you must have seen this already. If we can help you with anything, please say so.' 'Thank you Ann, can I say Ann?' 'Yes, of course, please take a seat!' 'If I am not interrupting anything?' 'No, not at all , my friend Lucy will join me shortly to have a glass of wine as well.' Ann looked around if she saw Lucy. She didn't. She turned her head to Donnah again and asked : 'How did you end up here, there are so many possibilities in the neighbourhood to spend your vacation. And cheaper options as well. The chalet of Rose is expensive to rent.' 'I saw an ad in a local newspaper back home. I don't like mass tourism at all and the rent is okay. It isn't that high, you see. The park has a swimming pool, a restaurant and last but not least most people are British, so it is kind of familiar .' 'That's very nice to hear, Donnah, and indeed we all know each other and help each other here. Don't forget the nice little shop of Debbie, you can buy fresh bread there every day.' Siobhan drank her glass of wine in one big gulp. At once she realized she shouldn't have done so, now she was not able to control herself completely, and she decided to leave. 'Thank you very much for your pleasant company, Ann. I really enjoyed it, please excuse me, I just arrived and I am still tired of the long journey,' she said politely. 'If you need anything, please let us know, it was nice meeting you too.' Siobhan walked to the chalet of Rose. 'So this is the murderer of my grandfather,' she thought. 'That woman has no idea what is in store for her.'

23.

'Samir, you need to join the 'cooking group' today. 'Today we are going to make couscous together. You must explain to the Dutch elderly group how important it is to have meals together in the Moroccan culture. In this way you contribute to an essential understanding of each other's habits and culture, you see?' I will report this in your file, that you did this activity,' Jody said. She was his coach during his internship in the elderly home 'The Close Encounter'. Samir didn't feel at ease. He didn't like to be in the kitchen, in his eyes it was the domain of women; to make dinner was the last thing on earth he wanted to do. 'That Jody is just another liberal fucking Dutch woman. Who does she think she is? That she could force him, he who was an important man in the Islamic network, into the kitchen?' But he had no choice. If he refused she would report his attitude to the college and this meant directly a meeting with arrogant van Balen and that terrible Kramer woman. With great reluctance he walked behind Jody to the kitchen. Jody was going to be another victim when the Great Islamic Empire would be a fact. He would put her in his file for sure. But for now he had to play the game and steal the show, the better this succeeded, the less attention he would draw. The kitchen of the elderly home was equipped with all facilities you could wish for; large modern stoves, ultramodern refrigerators, large kitchen sinks and cabinets stuffed with all sorts of fresh and canned food. This mixed elderly home populated with people from various cultural and ethnic backgrounds was meant to be an example. People could meet and get to know each other's culture, it was how the Dutch government thought the society was meant to be. The king himself had opened this home, accompanied by the queen. She was dressed in a colourful dress with an African motif and a traditional African hat. Of course it had been on tv. This was the future for all of Europe; to grow old in a multicultural community, put together in a modern and beautiful building. The children and grandchildren would visit their parents and grandparents together and they would meet each other in a special meeting room. When you start talking to each other the prejudices about one another will disappear, or so was the reasoning of the government. The 'Encounter' was subsidized by large sums of money of course. This project had to succeed. It had a clinic with physiotherapy, a pharmacy, a small hospital. There was a supermarket and a restaurant where you also could eat strictly halal. The people who were able to live in their own apartment with a hypermodern kitchen, could cook whenever they wanted. With an advanced communication system the staff could monitor the ones who needed a lot of care. A vicar worked there, too, as well as an imam, a priest and a humanistic counsellor. There were different rooms where you could pray, but there were also services for everyone together. They were held by the imam, priest, vicar and humanistic counsellors all together. These meetings were held in the central hall. The doctrine that was preached was that we all believe in the same God, but in our own way. Allah, God, Christ, or JWH, it was one and the same entity of love and understanding. The theory and practice of this special home attracted the attention of other countries around the world. Some politicians and elderly workers from Germany, Belgium and the UK had visited to see how they could implement this in their own country. The authorities in the Netherlands had the opinion they were setting an example again for the rest of the world like they had done in other matters before.

Jody introduced Samir to the group as being an excellent student who was very glad to do his internship in this elderly home. She said he was going to explain everything about making couscous and teach the whole group some Arabic words in relation to this particular meal. Everybody was welcome to ask Samir what he or she wanted, he was a person to be trusted. Samir looked at the old people who were sitting in a circle. Old women who were wearing a headscarf, old Dutch women who were dressed in a skirt which looked very youthful, some of the old men were dressed in a kaftan, some of them in a grey formal suit as if they wanted to give a signal that they had been important in society. But this only gave the impression of a lost world. 'Even men are being forced to join this charade,' Samir thought, 'It's really terrible.' Jody gave him a sign he had to say : 'It's so wonderful that we are cooking together in Arabic.' The group had to repeat this as a token of respect for people who spoke another language. Samir almost choked, as angry as he felt that he had to do this. As if he was a doll. A marionette that had to perform at command. When the meal was ready it was put on a cart. The group had dinner in a cosy room together. Samir's job was finished for today, before he left the building he went to the bathroom. Finally he could breathe a little bit. He had to hurry to the garage for his holy mission. One fine day everybody would have to bow for him. If that Johan, who thought he could fuck his own sister without punishment, and that arrogant van Balen would not shut up he knew another method of silencing them forever. A good method, too, with which the problem would be solved. He raced from the terrain, on to the street, not paying attention to the traffic. A car honked loudly. He threw his bike on the ground, entered the garage box quickly and closed the door right after him. He carefully moved the surfboard and lifted it from the transmitting device. The real thing had already started. That bitch from Northern Ireland was at her destination now to test the secret weapon, as soon as she would report, the big party could finally start. In the main shopping arear, at the Portuguese synagogue, in the City of London, the memorial site of the Twin Towers in New York, the secret weapon, the poison ball, would do its work without mercy everywhere. People would drop dead in an instant, everyone would wonder why, since the poison ball would have already disappeared. Total panic would be the result, government officials would not know how to respond, the City would be destroyed for once and for all. The first battle would be won and total chaos was going to be the outcome. From this mess a new Islamic Empire would rise. Samir was promised he was going to be a very important man in this new Empire, as a reward for his dangerous work for the 'Dawn of the True Islam'. Everybody had to obey HIM, not the other way around. He started up the transmitting device, that couldn't be traced by any normal satellite. This was held impossible by the 'Dawn.' He spoke again with his brothers in New York and London, about his worries concerning that Irish woman and her partner in crime, Sean. They knew way too much and could endanger the whole operation. In his opinion it might be an idea to kill them both as well with a small posion ball and totally destroy their bodies. The result of this would be simply that they would be 'missing'. But even then MI6 could start an investigation, and the link could be made with the real IRA. One way or another those two were a great risk. Samir asked if the cell in London and New York were able to solve this problem with him. In the end these people were nothing more than infidels, just dogs. Not even worth to spend a precious poison ball on, but this seemed to be the most effective method in the given circumstances. He felt an arousal in his loins. He longed for a real woman, an Islamic woman who, just as he did, believed in the holy Jihad and the founding of a Great Islamic Empire. A woman who would serve him and bear him many children. He was convinced that she already was walking the earth, but she hadn't revealed herself yet. But Allah would send her soon to him, he was sure of that.

24.

Siobhan was surprised how luxurious the chalet of Rose really was. It had a large bathroom, a modern open kitchen and a marble floor. After meeting her target she felt very tired. She was afraid she had said too much as a result of drinking the wine. But her cover up was also to behave like a normal tourist would do among the residents of the park. After her target was put out of action, she had to leave the country again as a regular tourist and fly back to London. Of course it was a risk when somebody died all of a sudden in this park, the local police could start an investigation. But on the other hand, it was nothing special. The park was full of elderly people who died because of old age, it was the natural course of things. Everybody knew this could happen. Siobhan opened her fridge. It was stuffed with food and wine.' 'I want to drink wine, wine.' She opened a bottle and started drinking, she had just met the woman who had mercilessly killed her grandfather, and destroyed the life of her father. She drank another glass of wine and another one, she hoped she would be able to sleep that night. There was a knock on the door. 'Now I need to play my role again.' She opened the door, it was Ann. 'Sorry Donnah, I hope I don't disturb you, but I would like to invite you for dinner tomorrow evening. My partner Lucy is attending a meeting with the local shooting club, and I am not interested in that at all.' 'Thank you for the invitation Ann, that is very kind of you, yes I would love to,' Siobhan said in her most upper class English accent. 'When do you expect me?' 'Around half past eight.' 'Where is your chalet exactly?' Ann gave her the directions and left in the dark, a heavy silhouette slowly disappearing. 'Now I have another problem, I have to have dinner with that creature. But if I had refused for sure the gossiping machine would have started, so I had no choice.' She opened her suitcase and grabbed her toilet bag. Standing in front of the mirror she saw a women with ugly dark patches under her eyes. Donnah Nugent didn't do her any good.

Lucy opened the door for Ann, she saw her wiggling in the dark, she hadn't her flashlight with her. 'Please sit down, Ann, I need to talk with you.' 'Nothing serious I hope?' 'That depends how you look at the matter altogether. No more excuses. I want you to go to that spiritual centre in Porto for a treatment. I am volunteering to go with you, so that it seems like we are going on a city trip to Porto.' Ann felt a sharp stab in her abdomen. She didn't want to go to Porto but stay close to Donnah, so she could look at her breasts, her lovely shape and the beautiful dress she was wearing, and to listen to her wonderful voice. 'I don't know Lucy, perhaps it is better to have another meeting with father Steve first.' 'Ann, you are running away again, no more excuses this time.' 'This week I'll stay in the park, next week my mind will be open for things like that, I promise.'

25.

As soon as that Irish bitch would set foot on English soil he would be notified directly. Samir was to be found in the garage box every day now. He had arranged to leave a bit earlier. He told Judy, his internship coach, that he was helping his parents with improving their Dutch. After thirty years of living in the Netherlands, their command of Dutch was still poor. His mother hardly spoke the language at all and could not write a proper sentence yet. Jody thought it was an excellent idea and gave him a big compliment: 'He was a very good example of the 'participation society'. This was a new concept launched by the Dutch government. The idea was that citizens should help each other instead of relying on help from the authorities, as had been the case for many years now. Judy promised to put a positive note in Samir's file. According to her, his was a good example for other young people. Even Mr. Van Balen and that stupid Kramer woman were happy about his attitude. So there was no suspicion from those quarters. He felt almost peaceful for a moment, laying on his bed in his very small room, in the flat of his parents on the eighth floor. He stared at the ceiling of his cubicle. In his thoughts he was drawing the outline of the New Empire of the True Islam. This empire would probably consist of Iraq, Saudi Arabia, Jordan, and Palestine as well as the Yemen. The Jews would be driven out and if they didn't leave they would all be exterminated. It could be enlarged later and include Egypt as well, Libya, Tunisia, Algeria, Morocco, Spain, and Portugal. Maybe even a part of France, until the Vichy line, the line drawn across the country from East to West. Major parts of Western Europe, countries like Germany, the Netherlands, Belgium, Great Britain, would become vassal states, just like the eastern European states had been in the time of the Soviet Union of old. Secret terror cells next to the one existing in New York had to be established in the USA, in African countries and Asia to prepare organized attacks with the poison ball, to create disorder, fear and destabilisation in all those societies. Of course the government of Indonesia would beg to join the Empire of the True Islamic State in the end. They would feel the pressure from the population to join in.

The new Empire was going to be controlled by the Caliph as an absolute ruler, directly below him there would be administrators who swore loyalty to him with their blood. Everywhere the sharia would reign; the Islamic law was going to be the basis for all constitutions. Those who didn't obey would be punished by corporal punishment, prison sentences and if you weren't loyal to Islam the death penalty. Everybody had to go to the Koran schools beside the normal but censured education. The history education would only present the true history of the great civilisation that Islam once was, and would be again, rising from the ashes of destruction. All women had to wear a niqaab, were not allowed to drive cars anymore, from the age of sixteen they were to be married off, after finishing school at that same age. It would make no sense to educate them any further since their role would be to serve their pious Muslim husbands, and to give birth to many children. Anyone who dared to disobey the new laws of The Empire, was sent to prison but also would be trained to improve him or herself. If this didn't work the death penalty would be executed in public, to serve as a deterring example. All communication systems like social media, radio, television, newspapers and magazines were to be controlled and only would serve the Islamic State. These would play a role in announcing new measures and spread the ideas of the 'True Islam'. If someone would use the media in any other way, he or she would get the death penalty instantly, without any form of trial whatsoever. Behind the scene in the of the 'Dawn of True Islam' new preparations were made every day. The most important terror cells in New York, Amsterdam, Libya and in London worked day and night to prepare for the new Empire. Thanks to their advanced communication system, they were able to communicate all over the World with each other without being noticed. For years they had worked on this new system without being noticed. The developers were trained at the best technical universities in the USA and Europe. Samir smiled, he was the humble student of social science at a simple college in Amsterdam, who had to obey stupid female college lecturers, he who had to cook in the kitchen, he who had to allow that his sister was dating a nonbeliever, would be the saviour of the 'True Islam' in the near future. He closed his eyes, unzipped his trousers. He touched his manlihood and ejaculated soon after. This was his semen, that once would fertilize his beautiful young woman with brown eyes, with beautiful breasts and long dark hair. He opened his eyes, with a simple click his television started. He had to follow the Dutch news for 'The Dawn' to see if there was any news about them. He had to monitor what they said about any terror threats in the Netherlands and other Western countries. He was following analysts who specialised in Islam in general, those of the Dutch secret service, the AIVD, in particular.

26.

Ann set the table, with the most beautiful tablecloth and tableware they had. Especially for this dinner she had polished her silver cutlery. She really looked forward to the time she was going to spend with this beautiful Donnah. She could do without the sharp comment from Lucy. Without any doubt she would soon notice that Ann was attracted to Donnah. Ann had bought a good bottle of port, a bottle of white and red wine which had cost nine euro each. This was very expensive for Portuguese wines, since one could buy a decent bottle of good wine for only two euro. She stood in front of the little mirror in her chalet. She had draped her fat body into a wide and bright blue dress which reached her ankles. This kind of dress you could buy anywhere near the beach. But with the glitter on the upper part it did look very good on her, Ann thought, it camouflaged her fat neck a bit in her eyes. The dark red lipstick flattered her face , not that she thought she had any sex appeal to Donnah, but nevertheless she wanted to look at her very best. Probably Donnah was a heterosexual, had a boyfriend, had a well paid job, was visiting fancy disco's and had a dynamic social life just like anybody at her age. But despite of this all, Ann wanted to look impressive in her own way, even if it was just for one evening. She heard a soft knock on the door. Ann opened the door and saw Donnah dressed in a beautiful pink dress, her dark brown hair in contrast to her white skin, two golden earrings in the shape of a drop of rain. She was wearing a flower on the right side of her head, in her hair. Ann was speechless for a moment, realizing she fell in love with Donnah at that same moment. But intuitively she knew this wasn't mutual. 'Donnah, you look fantastic, we welcome you to our chalet.' 'Thank you, I brought a little present for you.' She gave Ann a little box with chocolates, 'Made in Belgium' was written on the box. 'Thank you very much, but you didn't have to do this. Still, it is very kind of you, maybe we can taste some with our coffee after dinner.' 'Yes, please do so, your fat body will even die before I can test the secret weapon. What an ugly woman you really are,' Siobhan thought: 'Your fat arms look even worse in that terrible blue dress. But those arms won't have a long life anymore, very soon they'll stop moving.' 'Would you like to have a glass of wine, Donnah?' ' I would like to start with some mineral water if you don't mind?' Siobhan didn't want to drink wine too soon. It might influence her behaviour and that was a risk she couldn't take right now. 'With dinner a glass of wine, that's just fine with me,' she said. 'No problem, Donnah, you name it, I want to let you feel as comfy as I can, you are my guest.' Ann turned around to get a glass of mineral water for Siobhan, accidently she rubbed with her fat butt against Donnah's hip. Donnah almost had to throw up, but she controlled herself. 'I hope you like French onion soup, fillet of chicken and a fresh salad with olives?' 'Oh yes, I do. Tell me Ann, how did you end up in such a park in Portugal?' 'That is a long story, Donnah,' 'Well, I have the whole meal to listen to you.' 'That is really nice of you that you are interested, I hardly tell anyone my story nowadays.' She felt her body starting to glow again, Donnah who was interested in the story of old Ann. 'Let's eat some soup, please be seated,' she said. Donnah sat down at the table, curious what her target would say. Perhaps she would give her even more reason to get rid of her, with the help of the little poison ball. She took a small sip from her glass of wine. 'Cheers Ann, to a lovely evening,' she said. Ann raised her glass. 'May this be your last glass of wine, they probably have to order an extra wide coffin for you,' Siobhan thought. She tasted the onion soup, and took a bite of the French bread. At the same time she wanted to ask a question, she choked terribly. Ann patted her gently on her back and ended with a soft caress. Siobhan shuddered in disgust, but Ann felt it and thought it was a positive sign. As soon as Siobhan was able to speak again she said: 'I am curious what you are going to tell.' She hoped that Ann would move back to her chair, which she did. 'Where shall I begin?' 'Just start.' With great pleasure I am living here in the park. I have a lot of good English and Scottish friends. Unfortunately some people have had to sell their property, sometime because of health problems, sometimes people can't afford it anymore. By the way the British doctors are the best, no Portuguese can ever reach this level, but you understand this of course. These days the Dutch are buying our property in the park for no price at all, prices are much too low these days, the vultures have arrived, it is really terrible! I used to be a captain in the British army. Unfortunately I had to serve during 'The Troubles'. Of course you know Donnah, how difficult and hostile the Northern Irish people were towards us, these utterly ungrateful creatures. All we wanted to do was to spread peace and stability over there. They were even slaughtering each other, the poor souls. Every night I have nightmares about this, I found it terrible to be there. I was there you know, with Bloody Sunday. You know of course what this event was all about?' 'Yes I do, besides being a special needs teacher I give history lessons, too. British children need to know what happened over there, of course.' Siobhan didn't want to say much more, she was afraid that she couldn't control her emotions. 'I for sure have used my gun on that terrible day, but I am not sure if I hit someone, I really don't, believe me. Every time it's a different version of the same dream. A man is collapsing, one of his eyes is falling out of his head, a river of blood comes out of the hole, it has no end. Sometimes a child is holding his hand, he or she tries to shout, but no sound comes out of the mouth. I wake up every night bathing in my own sweat. I can't experience any inner peace any more. I am a prisoner of my dreams and my rotten past. I don't know if I really hit someone, I don't know if I destroyed anyone's life. In the park nobody knows anything about this, except Lucy, my partner of course, they only know I was stationed in West-Germany after World War Two. I don't know, Donnah, why I told you all of this, but please don't tell anyone, my life in the park would be over quite soon.' 'It's okay, Ann don't worry, it is awful that you can't come to terms with the past, and that you cannot find peace anymore, too.' She directly thought: I shouldn't have said the word 'too'. Ann didn't seem to notice it. 'I really like to tell you this in such a free manner, I tell you what really goes on in my mind. I hardly do that ever, you know how people can gossip very easily among one another in an English park in a foreign country like Portugal. Fortunately the Dutch and the Scandinavians in the park have really no clue what we are up to and talk about, at least this is positive. I don't understand those people at all, with their clothing which is too showy by far, their loud mouth and their rude manners. Really I don't understand them at all. That blonde Dutch woman named Paula van Walsum, she is wearing those tiny bikinis, they should forbid it in the park!' 'But we do know how to behave correctly, don't we Donnah.' Siobhan nodded. 'But child, what am I sitting talking, you must be very hungry, I'll put the chicken and salad on the table now, you must be starving!' As soon as Ann had put the food on the table, a large portion of everything did not go to Siobhans plate, and she wasn't even asked how much she wanted. 'No wonder that you are so fat,' she thought. After she had eaten a bit, Ann put more food on her plate at once. Siobhan carefully looked around in the chalet, she wanted to find a suitable spot to lay down the little poison ball, later during the week. After it spread its deadly poisonous gas which could not be smelled, it would disappear and vanish for ever. It would seem as if the person had died a natural death. This person might be examined to find out about the cause of death. The test would be a real success if no trace of the poisonous gas would be found. This was still a matter of concern. The little balls were different in size, it depended on the occasion for which they were to be used. A bigger one for a large crowd in a large hall or a whole building, a smaller one for one or two persons in an office. In this kind of terrorist attack it was not necessary to destroy whole buildings with a heavy bomb. In the end it was essential to kill people and their ideas, philosophies, cultures and their whole societies. Buildings were only dead material and of no value in itself.

Ann saw that Donnah smiled. 'Child, have another glass of wine, that will do you good,' she said. Without asking she poured wine in Siobhan's glass. 'Now I am curious about you, I've heard in the park you are living in the northern part of London?' 'That is not the best part of London to live in, no wonder you need a few weeks' vacation,' she said with a wink, which gave Siobhan a feeling of pure disgust. 'For me it's okay to live there, I have some very friendly Pakistani neighbours really, they take care of my plants and look after my flat, while I am on this holiday and enjoying your company. My work as a special needs teacher is really interesting, you can make the difference for some kids who need a little extra attention. 'We do have the best educational system in the world, Donnah, be proud you can contribute with your special skills.' 'It's the way you look at it,' she thought, she had to bite her tongue not to speak out and say what she really thought about this. 'You know you can always ask us for help if you need anything, how long are you going to stay?' 'I can only stay fourteen days, no longer. My pupils and the school need me, you see.' 'Well, I've heard that you had mentioned a month, but oh the people just gossip a lot.' 'I know this Ann, and that is why it's better that I leave now. I am a little tired, but thank you very much for the wonderful dinner.'

Without saying anything more she walked to the door opened it and disappeared in the dark. Ann felt deeply surprised that Donnah left so suddenly. She felt really disappointed and realized that there was no chance to be alone anymore with Donnah. Lucy was around all the time, in the park somebody would be watched all the time by one or another. Most likely, all she could do was take a peek at that beautiful young woman she fell in love with. Suddenly she felt very tired, realizing she had given away her deeply kept secret to Donnah, without knowing who she really was. What on earth did she know about this Donnah? Practically nothing. From now on she had to control herself again and pay attention once more. Lucy was right, there was no excuse anymore for not going to Porto to work on the past, to finally find some inner peace again. Ann walked towards the sink to wash the dishes. All of a sudden she felt old, very old indeed.

27.

Kramer, mister Van Balen of the college where Samir studied and Jody, the coach of his internship, were seated opposite Samir. He had to attend and couldn't escape from the 'very serious conversation' they wanted to have with him. He hadn't a clue why, his internship didn't lead to any problems that he knew of. The elderly people liked him, Jody had commented positively on his 'work attitude' and his commitment to work with various people in general. 'What now?,' Samir thought. He hardly could control an urge to throw up. What a lot of bullshit, to want to 'coach' and control him again and again. He felt very sick. How many times he had to go through this again? And he also had to be very thankful to them, they invested so much time in him. Why in heavens' name didn't they keep a check on more students from the white population of the Netherlands? 'As if they were totally perfect themselves! Why in the name of Allah did they always focus on him? Or did he have the wrong ideas in his head?' He did not have time to reflect, because the cross examination was to begin. 'Samir,' Judy said: 'We are very satisfied with your internship so far. The elderly people like you very much, you do contribute to our ideal, that people of different cultural background should mix. We decided that you can have a word with our queen when she will visit our home. I can't give you the details yet, when she is going to visit us exactly etcetera. The AIVD has screened you, and nothing special was found. Our home has the special attention of the queen and our king. As you know he opened it not long ago. Especially our queen is now very interested in our example setting project. The next few weeks you'll get a special training, so that you can talk to the queen in an appropriate way and show her how you do your job here as a Moroccan student. I am sure she will be very pleased. Of course this event will be reported on television, so you'll get a media training as well. We can't afford to make any mistakes of course, this is a chance to get some positive news coverage. My question is, are you aware what important task you have to perform?' 'Yes ma'am it's great honour to meet our queen, I will try my very best.' He closed his eyes for a second. 'Fine, we are all counting on you. It is also a good opportunity for you to get a job more easily after you finish your education at the college. This is his last internship before his last paper, isn't it, mister van Balen? Did I understand this correctly?' 'Yes, this is correct. Young man, this is the chance of a life time. If your media performance is successful you'll get a job in no time and this is very precious these days.' 'Can I ask a question?' 'Go ahead, Samir,' Jody said. 'If you are so satisfied about me, why can't I get a job here right away?' 'I can't exclude this when you graduate successfully. Now let us close this meeting. You know what to do the rest of day?' 'Yes madam.' He left the room and walked to the recreation hall. Together with the women who worked that day he had to guide a group of Somalian, Dutch, Moroccan and Hindustani old women with their special 'game afternoon'. His shoulders were sagging. Now he had a problem, a very big problem, the Dutch Secret Service had screened him, until now they hadn't found anything against him, but you never knew what the near future might bring. On the other hand the whole operation of the 'Dawn of True Islam' was in full swing now and it wasn't noticed, so this could be a positive sign as well. It seemed they could even function under the umbrella of the AIVD now. He opened the recreation hall. He had to put all sorts of games on the table before the women entered. Some of them called him 'Sami' , really liked him and told him their life stories and grabbed his hand for a moment, as if he were their favourite grandson.

28.

Despite the wonderful weather Siobhan was hardly able to enjoy it. Again and again she had to remind herself to play her role of Donnah in a perfect way. This was almost too heavy for her. She saw the deep blue spots beneath her eyes getting darker and darker every evening. The story of Ann had made a deep impression on her. This woman seemed to suffer for what she had done in the past, just as her own family did. It was very difficult for Siobhan not to allow herself these feelings. She had to say to herself time and again that this was a target to kill, to test the poison ball, nothing more. That woman had to be killed, rather sooner than later. In addition she would serve her mother organisation, the real IRA. After a successful try out they were able to hit several targets in the City of London. Great Britain was to be hit hard, right in its heart. Perhaps she was also scheduled for other assignments of the 'Dawn', she didn't know about that yet. No feelings of any sort could be allowed now, no way. The people in the park had been very friendly to her so far. They had more than once offered her to do the groceries in Tavira for her, since she didn't have car. When she walked in the direction of Manta Rota to go the beach, a car from the park would stop to offer her a lift. Everybody invited her to participate in all sorts of games, being

British she really belonged to the group. Those simple friendly people had no idea what was going to happen in the near future. But she had to go ahead as planned, if she didn't either the real IRA or the 'the Dawn of the True Islam' would kill her as a traitor who posed a great danger to both organisations. But not only that, her family would be in trouble as well. There was no other way out than to test the poison ball and leave quickly afterwards. She wished this was all behind her. Everything that had to take place was approaching almost too fast for her liking. She had already noticed the perfect spot to lay down the miniscule poison ball in the chalet. Ann had asked her more than once, inviting her for a cup of tea, or a glass of wine with Lucy and herself. There would be enough opportunities to put it where she wanted, in an unguarded moment. That shouldn't be a problem at all. If Lucy was lucky the little ball would do its devastating work when she wasn't in the chalet. If not she only was going to be collateral damage, no more. In the long term picture the individual was totally subordinate to the major turn in history. An essential turn in history was very near, one that would influence mankind as a whole in the future. Siobhan actually just wanted to sleep the next few days, do her thing and leave for Faro. But this was impossible, the residents would notice this and start gossip about 'beautiful Donnah from the northern part of London.' That's how she was called now in the park : 'beautiful Donnah'. But this Donnah didn't feel beautiful inside at all. She felt a mix of blind hatred, supressed anger most of the time, but also felt a kind of pity for Ann, the woman who was too big for a normal sized coffin. She imagined a dead Ann lying in the coffin, Lucy bending over her face with tears in her eyes. The park would be totally upset about another sudden death of a resident, cause unknown.

She had lived an unhealthy life, so on the other hand her death could not be a big surprise, that woman was going to die soon anyway. Siobhan poured herself another glass of wine, hoping she would be able to sleep tonight. Lately she had trouble falling asleep, this influenced her concentration during the day, it was very unpleasant but even more so endangering her mission. Her head was spinning, her body felt very heavy. She sweated heavily and felt like a prisoner of the situation she had partially created herself. Siobhan was not allowed to have any doubts, but she did have them. If Ann was dead, was it really possible for her to feel relief? That finally the past was put behind them. For one moment she wished she had listened to her father's advice, to leave the past for what it was and focus on the future. Probably she would be teaching about the Roman Empire at the very same moment, trying to explain the complexity of its political system. She realized she missed her pupils, their moods, their sense of humour, but their loyalty towards her the most. Her cover up was a study trip to Italy and now and then a postcard from the square of St. Peter or the Colosseum was sent home. It was permitted to call once during this fortnight, she had a special code on her mobile to do so. But until now she didn't feel like it, to tell another fake story. During her mission there was no direct contact with the untraceable network of the 'Dawn'. Even though normal communication systems couldn't discover it, you never knew a hundred percent certain and the secret services were not sitting on their hands doing nothing. As soon as she set foot on British soil again Sean had to be informed directly, to report to the terror cell in London. Perhaps this whole revenge plan wasn't such a good idea after all. Perhaps revenge wasn't an answer, and didn't solve anything and would only leave total emptiness behind. Although she really was disgusted, not only by the appearance of Ann, especially the unwanted touching of her, she was a human being too, with a partner. She seemed to be appreciated by the fellow residents for her contribution to the community of the park. Siobhan had not expected she was also wrestling with the past. She didn't let go of the past, nor did the past let go of her. She had expected an arrogant and indifferent English stuck up woman, who lived without any worries under the Portuguese sun. Not being aware she had destroyed lives. This was not the case, Siobhan realized now even more so, but it was no option to cancel her mission. It was very easy to realize what the plans of the 'Dawn' and the real IRA would be regarding her person. If she was going to be captured by one of the secret services, she would be a magnificent catch, knowing everything she did. This also meant captivity for a very long period, not a very pleasant future to look forward to. 'Another fine mess I got myself into,' she thought, thinking of the famous remark by Laurel and Hardy. Yes, a bigger mess wasn't possible, for why in heavens' name did she agree to have dinner with that Ann woman?' Curiosity? Or was this a part of her assignment to behave as a tourist and to be British among the British? Actually, she was a guinea pig herself, since both organisations wanted to see if it was possible to leave Portugal again as normal tourist, after the poison ball did its work and vanished forever. Blind hatred had driven her until now, she even didn't like the fact anymore that on the outside she was perfect in control of her feelings, or else the mission would not have gone through at all. She felt anger, her father never had been able to express his feelings towards her, although he loved her very much, chained to his traumas of the past. That woman here in Portugal was protected by law, living here in Portugal a comfortable life under the circumstances. She hated that woman who had protected the Orangemen, who treated her and her family as a peace of shit. She had to die, the sooner the better.

29.

Samir was sitting at his computer. The video images were moving fast in front of his eyes. An imam was preaching, he called for Holy War against the pernicious Western countries and their values. He called on young people to convert to the True Islam, to pray to Allah the Highest, to abandon worldly matters and to join in the holy jihad. Every Muslim had to do so, and die if need be for the Holy War. Since Samir had learned perfect Arabic during his Koran lessons at the mosque, he understood every word of what the imam said. He had his headphones on, he didn't think anyone could hear what he was listening to. The imam repeated his call for a devout life, there was no other way. With one click he changed channels, he knew the sites where the True Islam was preached. On this site it was explained how devious the Western countries really were, everyone had to convert to Islam, the sharia had to become the basis for official law in every country as soon as possible. An imam explained that democracy only kept people from serving Allah. Once all democracies with Allah's help would become true Sharia states in the near future. He called up on all Muslims in the world to prepare these sharia states and to commit coordinated terror attacks on vital elements of the Western societies, for this was the will of Allah. All Christian symbols were to be destroyed. Church towers would be replaced by minarets, like a sort of contemporary iconoclasm. Finally after the long Christian period there was going to be a Greater Islamic Empire again everywhere. This Christian and dominant culture had now come to an end. The imam also warned against the influence of the Jews, their power in the future Islamic society had to be broken totally, in the new order a kind of slaves' role would be their fate. If they didn't obey and convert, the death penalty would be their end. Samir felt very proud he was part of this important turn in History itself. Finally his mask of college student belonged to the past. The people who had hurt him the most, like that terrible woman Kramer, arrogant Van Balen, were to be punished by him and his brothers in faith. But at first they had to bend for him. Jody, who was also a freethinking Dutch bitch of course, would receive a milder punishment, she wasn't the worst person on earth. She had to become his housekeeper, serving him and his wife. Just like serving a queen and a king she had to leave the room walking backwards. He and his wife would have a wonderful devout life serving Allah, living for a higher goal, with prayer, and contemplation, so they could help and lead the whole world towards Him. Still he was a bit worried that he was honoured to have this conversation with the queen, the Dutch secret service the AIVD didn't find anything which pleaded against him, but this could happen still, you never knew. On the other hand he felt grateful they had checked him and nothing was found. Apparently they did not know he was connected to 'The Dawn of True Islam' and the terror attacks which were being prepared. Of course the king and his fashionable queen were unbelievers, too, who might play a minor role in the New Empire, what to do with them wasn't clear yet.

30.

A hand was put on her mouth, she almost choked and felt terribly scared. She wanted to shout, but no sound came out of her mouth. Her body was totally rigid now. Her mouth was taped, a huge cap was put over her head. 'This is the end,' she thought, 'I am going to die, either the real IRA or 'the Dawn' doesn't trust me any longer. She was surprised that she could still think clearly after the first fright. She was thrown over the shoulder of a big man. The person walked about fifty yards, she estimated. During her training in Libya this had been a drill, too: if she was abducted she had to notice every detail and remember them as best as she could, sounds, distances, the language she heard, the sounds of vehicles of any kind. She heard a door was opened. It was probably the door of a van. Someone put her down on a stinking mattress. An engine started. No word was spoken. After driving about an hour on a road with holes, probably secondary roads, the vehicle stopped. Siobhan was put on a sort of stretcher by two persons. The thing was shoved into something else. Ear protectors were put on her head. With high speed the vehicle lifted from the ground. She lost consciousness after she got an injection. The crew of the aircraft started talking to each other again. Of all people, David was the co-pilot on this special flight. He just notified the control tower in Faro that the aircraft was on its way to Tel Aviv. The Israelis had special permission of the government of Portugal to carry out this secret mission, the Portuguese were informed up to a certain level, for the Israeli authorities wanted to inform them. The Portuguese however had a sense of urgency about the whole matter. David felt quite insecure, seeing Siobhan like this, under these circumstances. He had taken a big risk, and so did she, to meet each other in private during their stay in Amsterdam. The attraction had been mutual and very strong, that much was clear. He still felt attracted to her even in the given situation. He looked at her beautiful pale face for a second, she seemed so vulnerable. 'Shalom, how are you?' They were flying over Cyprus now, estimated time of arrival is twenty minutes, we have a special load with us. The lights of Limassol were shining in the clear sky below them. When they landed safely near Tel Aviv Siobhan would be taken to a military hospital straight away. First she was going to be physically examined from top to toe. If she was fit enough it would be followed by conversations with a special psychiatrist who had dealt already for a long time with people who turned radical one way or another. Then the Mossad would continue the interrogation, this could become very tough. If she was willing to cooperate her life would take a very different course, if she didn't she would be either kept in prison until she decided to cooperate or perhaps be left on her own. This idea was unbearable for David. But he had hope, the investigation of the Mossad revealed she was not only very intelligent, but she had a passion for music as well, and was devoted to her students, may be this might save her. Although she was tough and managed to survive many difficult situations, she was also very vulnerable, with a traumatic family history. He knew from experience what this meant, as a large part of his family in the previous generation had been murdered in Auschwitz. This wound never healed, it seemed, and for generations it marked you in your whole being. The control tower gave a sign to start the descent. David looked at the instruments. The cruising altitude with its stable layers, was going to be left for lower altitude which most of the time was less stable. Every time David experienced it as a miracle when the aircraft safely touched the earth, although he knew this type of plane very well. It had never failed him.

31.

'We hope you rested a bit after your journey, miss O'Connor. I hope you had enough to eat and to drink? During the medical examination it showed there is nothing wrong with you physically. Your psychiatrist noticed you are very intelligent and you have no mental disorders. You are totally responsible for your deeds, we think. We know your family history, your background, and we know exactly with which Islamic organisation the real IRA is collaborating now. We examined the poison ball, we know precisely how it works, no doubt about this. You either can work with us, and with this cooperation prevent that thousands, maybe hundreds of thousands of innocent victims will die, or you don't. The total consequences will be for yourself. In reality this means either you will be shot by the real IRA, or by the 'Dawn of True Islam' as they call themselves. They will kill you for sure, personally I would prefer to be killed by the real IRA. You can ask us all sorts of questions, how we got our information, we won't answer you. It is classified and top secret. When you decide to cooperate with us, we offer you lifelong protection, training, education, a de-radicalisation programme with a specialized psychiatrist, an intensive course of Modern Hebrew and a permanent permit to live in Israel. As a cover up it may even be possible to teach here, after you have learned the language sufficiently. How we discovered what you were up to and where you were operating, don't ask. We won't answer, it's classified as military and a State secret. Concerning your family we only can say they will be protected as well, and in the future there can be limited contact with them, we will explain this in a later phase. But you can never tell the real reason why you are in Israel to your parents, for them it will seem you converted to Judaism and found your destiny here. It never will be allowed to emigrate anywhere else in the world, you understand? You will be under supervision of the Mossad for the rest of your life here. If you agree you'll remain our informant. You can sign for this. We'll bring you to a special room where you can think about our proposals, not more than an hour, if you decide to sign you also have a lifelong duty to be silent about all information we give to you. If you violate this rule, the consequences are for yourself, you will be left on your own, literally walking on the streets somewhere in Asia. Now follow us to the special contemplation room, we'll give you the documents to read. Siobhan had to follow two men and two women in army fatigues. One of the women opened the door of the room, where she had an hour to think about what had been said, and to read the documents. The room wasn't very big, three walls had light yellow colour. One wall had a window, she assumed on the other side they could see every move she made. She felt like a fish in an aquarium after the door was locked. She looked at the grey overall she was dressed in after the medical examination. There was no way out, even if she wanted to find a way out. She imagined she had seen David in a split second, the time they had spent together felt like it happened in another universe. She had felt so at ease with him, she had felt so beloved. But if it was David or not she had seen on the way, the situation she was in now was very complex. The decision before her had not only consequences for her own life, but also for her family, the school where she worked, her pupils which she would never see again, her life in Northern Ireland which would be over forever if she decided to stay in Israel and cooperate with the Mossad, the Israeli secret service. She wished her father was here to give her advice.

32.

Donnah Nugent was the talk of the town in the park for days on end. No one understood why she had left so suddenly, leaving a little bag at the reception with money as payment of the rent for the chalet of Rose. A little note was left saying: 'For the rent of the chalet'. This was not the way people treated each other in the park, it hurt the whole community. That was the opinion you could hear everywhere. An official complaint was made by Ann to the man who was in charge of daily matters, named Antonio. She made it very clear that not just anybody should be able to rent a chalet anymore, as this would mean insecurity for all of the residents. She was very surprised that Donnah had disappeared so suddenly out of her life again. Donnah had been a very pleasant break, away from her daily routine. For her it was a surprise she still was able to feel sexual arousal because of another person. At her age of sixty four, with all the discomfort she experienced, this was an eye opener. Meeting Donnah had enlightened her existence. Her disappearance was a mystery and she simply assumed she would never see her again. Lucy didn't want to be a witness of Ann's sleepless nights any more, walking up and down and smoking in the chalet. It became too much for her, she insisted on making an appointment with the spiritual healing centre in Porto very soon. They had already told everybody in the park that they were going to make a trip to the wonderful city of Porto. A few people asked them to make a lot of pictures, so they could show those to everyone in the park later on. While Ann got the treatment in the centre, Lucy was going to explore the city and stay in a small hotel. Ann would join her there after the treatment. A few pictures of them together in Porto and the cover up was complete. Lucy really hoped that Ann would respond positively to the hypnotherapy which seemed a good treatment for her. Maybe she would finally get rid of her repeating nightmares and her feelings of guilt which ruined her life in Portugal and not only her life. It had a deep impact on the life of Lucy as well.

Ann packed her suitcase. After she enrolled in the programme she had received an email with instructions which clothes were appropriate to wear during the sessions, for instance a jumpsuit and a bandanna.

To her dismay Ann read that smoking and drinking alcohol was forbidden on the grounds. The meals were purely vegetarian, with fresh fruit juices and special tea to cleanse the body. Ann wondered what kind of people she was going to meet in the group sessions. These were an important part of the therapy: to speak with others about your problems, your difficult past or what was bothering you. The idea was that you would understand that many people were living with a big burden on their shoulders. As a result your loneliness could be broken. Ann felt very nervous already, that she would have to share her well-kept secret of the past in a group as part of her therapy. She closed her suitcase, in a quarter of hour they were going to leave. Jeff offered to take them to the railway station of Vila Nova de Cacela. They decided to leave their own car at the chalet. She wondered how the world would look like when they returned to the park. Maybe she would sleep again normally, maybe she would have gotten rid of the nightmares, maybe she could close the matter forever and forgive herself. Suddenly the image of Donnah popped up in her head, she felt her whole body glowing. Why did Donnah disappear in heavens' name? Was there something the matter with her? Perhaps something had happened to her relatives in England. Ann inspected her handbag: her passport, her favourite perfume and her spray against the heat. 'Jeff arrived to pick us up,' Lucy said. 'Hello ladies, please enter my old coach.' With a little bow he opened the door, Jeff was always seeing the sunny side of life. 'I hope you have a great time in Porto. I envy you both, going to such a wonderful city! But we do all expect a load of photos and lots of stories and maybe a presentation for everyone.' Oh, my goodness,' Ann thought, 'now they expect a presentation at the bridge club, the petanque club, the quiz commission and the bingo group as well.' She hoped that Jeff would forget what he had just said. The car slowly descended the steep hills to the small station of Vila Nova de Cacela. The train was always on time, and if this wasn't the case a spontaneous strike had started. Or it could be a celebration of a local saint most tourists didn't know about. However this did not happen too often. Jeff stopped the car, Lucy and Ann said goodbye to him. They walked to the platform on the other side of the train station where no one was working anymore. Recently some men had painted the station white again, using bright blue colours on the edges, this way most of the white houses were decorated in Portugal. But it was a mess all around the train station, with garbage spread everywhere, not only near the little garbage can. The end of the platform was torn to bits, it all gave a poor impression as if there was no money left to maintain the rest. A few people waited for the train to arrive. An old woman wore an old fashioned dress with apron, she tried to start a conversation with Ann and Lucy. Lucy tried to say in the few words she knew in Portuguese that they didn't understand her. A bell rang in the distance. It was the sign the train to Faro was coming soon. They had booked a flight with TAP, the national Portuguese airliner, to Porto, the trip by train would be too exhausting for both of them. The train stopped, Ann and Lucy pulled themselves up the stairs. The whistle blew, the train started moving and its silhouette disappeared in the distance.

33.

'The suspect, Samir C., was described by one of his teachers mister Van Balen as a very cooperative student, his internship was marked as excellent until now. That Samir C. was suspected of preparing terrorist attacks was a shock to all of his teachers and his coach, Judy ten Have, at the elderly home. No one had ever expected this of him. In the elderly home, called 'The Close Encounter' where all kind of elderly people of different ethnic background lived, everybody had loved Samir C.. They were fond of him, the news that Samir C. might be part of an international terrorist network was a big shock to them all,' the news presenter said. 'We are going to report live now. Our special reporter John van Gelen is standing in front of the college where Samir C. is a student. In one shot the college filled the screen. John van Gelen asked a stout man in a grey suit: 'You didn't have a clue of the plans of your student Samir C., who was planning a terrorist attack, mister Van Balen?' 'Well, first of all this isn't clear yet. He is an unobtrusive student. His results in his internship were excellent, there were no problems at all. We gave him a lot of coaching and he comes from a hardworking taxpaying family. His parents watched over him, but gave him also freedom to participate in Dutch society. His sister and brother are excellent students, too. You can't blame his parents for anything.' 'Obviously those people were not aware of his plans, mister Van Balen,' John van Gelen said. 'Nor you and his coaches at his internship, can you explain this?' 'A lot is not yet very clear about all facts, so let's find out first what he did or didn't do. We don't know if he is part of a terror network, we shouldn't jump to conclusions yet, mister van Gelen.' 'So you think this poor student shouldn't be arrested even though the authorities have strong indications that he might be a member of a terrorist organization?' 'These are your words, mister van Gelen, I have no more comment at this moment.' The news reporter said: 'With this we end the coverage on this item, more about this matter in 'One Today'. 'Now for the weather report, what is it going to be, Simon?' Simon put a lovely summer's day on the screen, with high temperatures for the time of the year, September in the living rooms of Dutch fairy tale land. With a tablecloth and fresh flowers on the table, terror attacks were so far away from the Dutch dykes. A new TV programme was announced 'One Today'. 'Good evening ladies and gentlemen. In a flash the topics which were to been seen passed by.

The 'case Samir C. ' the AIVD, the Dutch Secret Service, the Israeli Mossad, the liberal mosque, which the parents of Samir attended, a garage box, mister Van Balen, Judy ten Have, the liberal imam and the principal of the college 'The Horizonten' where Samir C. was a student. In the end a psychiatrist would give an outline, what kind of a person a young terrorist could be. The prime minister and all political leaders didn't want to give any comment yet on the whole case, in their view it was too early for that. Only the right wing Dutch politician Geert Wilders would like to say something, but no one dared ask his opinion at this stage.

Samir C. was introduced to the public on TV as being a quiet student, nothing special, very much appreciated by the elderly people in the multicultural home where he worked as an intern. Being part of an everyday Islamic family that was totally integrated in Dutch society, there never had been any problems. A simple hardworking family it was, connected to a modest mosque with a totally integrated imam. Samir C. was selected by his excellent behaviour to meet the queen during her visit at the elderly home, where all sorts of people of different ethnic background lived in total harmony with each other. He had been screened by the Secret Service and nothing was found against him. The journalist of One Today said there was a suspicion that the Dutch Secret Service was tipped by the Israeli Secret Service, the Mossad. The AIVD in the Netherlands didn't want to comment on this, the official statement was : 'Because of the whole national and international safety situation, they couldn't give any comment'. His parents didn't want to appear on TV either. Jody told Samir C. was a wonderful student, loved by everyone, no one had ever expected this, no one. The imam of the liberal mosque did give comment, however. He stated that the mosque had an open and tolerant atmosphere, he never noticed anything special about Samir C., who was a normal young man. According to him the youth had every opportunity to talk with a special 'youth social worker' who was at the mosque every Tuesday and Thursday afternoon until nine o'clock in the evening. If they had any problems at school, work or internship this special islamic 'youth workers' couldn't only listen but also help with solving a problem, if necessary. Samir visited these meetings sometimes, nothing special was ever noticed; the same thing with his sister and brother. The mosque had nothing to hide, they said, and the TV crew could film the hypermodern interior with no limitations.

Mister Van Balen appeared again on TV. 'Mister Van Balen, if I am correct you had a special conversation with Samir C. before he went on his internship?' 'If I am well informed he was rejected two times before?' 'I don't exactly remember, mister van der Kley. For the job in the multicultural elderly home he was the perfect candidate for sure, he really knows how to work with elderly people very well and he was very patient with them all, they were fond of him, too. He did his homework always on time and his parents were looking after him.' 'I don't think so, sir, they didn't have any idea about what he was doing in the garage box of his.' She showed the garage box and its location in a nearby neighbourhood. The comment was that there was a hunch this might be the place where part of the preparation of terror attacks had taken place, it could not be verified yet, no one wanted to comment. Mister Van Balen kept on chatting about the fact that 'Samir C. was so friendly to his fellow students at the college'. At the very last moment the college decided to give no more comment on TV. 'It would disturb the other students too much'. 'Van Balen has said enough about the matter'. They gave an explanation for their sudden change of mind. The principal hoped that peace would return to the school, to all students and teachers. The journalist van der Kley commented: 'Colleges are once more denying the real situation, nothing new here, we have seen cases like this before…'

34.

Siobhan had limited time to make up her mind. She wondered if she really had any choice at all. If she was going to be released from this situation, this would mean her death sentence. Either the real IRA or the 'Dawn of the True Islam' would not rest until they had killed her one way or another. Nowhere on this planet she would be safe anymore; living as a hunted animal for the rest of her life. She simply knew too much. Maybe this was her destiny, to help to dismantle terrorist organisations in Israel. She had had her doubts already, if taking revenge on someone who killed a family member would give any relief at all. It seemed like it only exhausted her to think about it all the time. She tried to stand up and walk around a little bit in the room, but sat down again. Her vision became blurred, she remembered the wise words of her father again, that she should let go of the past. Would she ever see her father and her mother again? She wasn't in any situation to negotiate or to demand for privileges to those who held her in custody. Perhaps these new circumstances could offer her a new direction in life. Perhaps it was wise now to let go of the past, live in the present and possibly have a future of her own. Did she ever want to have children? Would it be possible to marry in this country? The door was opened. Two men and women accompanied her to another room. It was made clear to her that she had to sit down. A carafe filled with water and a holder with the Israeli flag stood in front of her on the table. 'Would you like a glass of water, miss O'Connor?' 'Yes, I would love to have one, thank you.' She drank it very quickly, she was thirsty. The room was all silent for a minute, as is if it was a holy moment. She opened her mouth and asked: 'Am I allowed to ask a question?' 'A relevant question is always welcome, please go ahead.' 'If I'll agree with your plan and I sign the papers, can I get married here? Can I have children of my own if I am healthy and all? You see I am still very young, and I am trying to imagine how my life would be here when I live here. In Ireland one's family life with children is very important so to say. I know I can't ask for much given the whole situation I am in.' 'We understand your question miss O'Connor. If your integration, learning the language, the habits of the country and the culture and the history of Israel is successful and you prove to be a loyal citizen as well as a worker for us, we don't see why not. Perhaps you get blessed after you get married.' We also think it's good that you participate in our society, start teaching again as a cover up for your work for us, the more normal your life seems here the better. 'I thought about it all, I can make a long story short, but I will sign. I see no alternative in my life at this point'. 'Okay, if you sign you will get a total new identity as you could read in the papers. Your new name will be : Hannah Yael Yvon. Your first name is a symbolic gift to you from us, since your Irish name is Siobhan which means : Johanna. Your last name is going to be a neutral one : Daran. We'll talk about all specific details with you later, with your new identity belong goes a different history. Your family back home have to experience restrictions as well, if they want to visit you this will happen in our house in Milan, later we'll tell all specific terms and conditions. Your parents have been screened by us and they seem reliable people to us, who really care for their daughter. 'I want to sign,' Siobhan said. They gave her a form, she didn't read it although it was in English, she just put her autograph on it at the bottom. A woman with a black ponytail nodded at her, and said: 'For the time being you'll stay here and get your own large room. Our special psychiatrist is going to have conversations with you every day. An intensive language program with a very good teacher is at your service to learn Modern Hebrew very quickly, you get a special training about the Jewish culture, history and our school system in Israel. Your new identity has to become your second nature. Besides of this all there is another interrogation about all that you know concerning the knowledge you have, so it will focus on both of the terror organisations you worked for. Any little detail you remember could be of great value. We have to hurry since we expect terror attacks very soon and have no time to lose. We will escort you to your room now. You can rest if you want for two hours, after that we'll start the first interrogation session.' The door of her room was locked. Siobhan fell asleep.

35.

'I assume the therapy did help you?' Lucy asked. 'You are so quiet, what on earth did they do to you over there?' It must be a trustworthy centre otherwise father Steve never would have sent you there. But why don't you say anything, Ann?' Ann was staring in front of her, looking a bit gloomy. What could she say? My whole life has been one big lie? I've always believed in total nonsense? I could have forgiven myself a long time ago, as this all belonged to my 'Karma'? My ego was hurt and I just wanted to please it, to feel less hurt? I denied my true destination in my life until now? 'I don't know where to start Lucy, to tell you the truth.' 'Well, you can try it anyway.' 'Okay, I'll tell my story, but don't expect too much of me.' For a moment she was silent, as if it had to be this way. Ann looked around at the terrace, which was situated near the riverside. It was filled with people who seemed to enjoy their life. Lucy was very curious about what Ann had to tell. Even though the hotel was beautiful, she had stayed on her own for a few days, and she was very glad Ann was with her again from now on. Ann opened her mouth: 'I got a bizarre feeling at the arrival. The spiritual centre is a kind of fake castle with towers, a few fountains in a big pond in front of it. It was as if I entered Disney

World. They welcomed me with a bow at the bottom of a flight of stairs, as if I was somebody very important. The stairs gave entrance to a huge marble hall. Soft music came from hidden loudspeakers. I got a single bedroom with a large window on one side, you could see the seashore at the end of the range of hills. The building has a bright yellow colour in the public areas, it gave me a light feeling from the beginning. After an hour they knocked on my door, it was time for the first session with an assistant of the yogi. During the session I was lying on a very comfortable deck chair. The room had different colours, soft rose, light yellow, lime green and a soft pink colour. I do remember I fell asleep but at the same time it felt like being wide awake. I heard a baritone voice that said over and over again: 'Bloody Sunday, Bloody Sunday, Bloody Sunday.' I saw the same image again: the man who collapsed, a little boy holding his hand. After that I could see a bright entity, a form or a spirit, I don't know exactly how to describe it. It said to me without any sound ; 'I have forgiven you. Go on with your life, love the people around you, show them your love by your deeds.' The spirit became vague. I was blinking my eyes and I woke up slowly, but like I told you I didn't feel awake at all, it was like dreaming, in a deep sleep. I got a very peaceful feeling inside. Something else I should mention, the food was delicious in the centre. Healthy salads, all sorts of herbal tea and no meat at all, nor any alcohol. They told us we poison our body every day, with food containing artificial colours and a range of other additives, with meat that is full of hormones, too much salt and sugar in almost everything we consume.

When you eat more healthily, it isn't only your body that is purified, your mind will be cleansed as well. Every morning before breakfast we did a meditation session together, with a sort of sound bowls, a very special experience for me. I felt so much inner peace I never experienced this in my life.' 'But how about the group sessions Ann, you were so much afraid of those?.' 'The first session was terrible, I can't deny it. We were a small group of four persons. I remember a story of a woman, she was telling that she had been neglected as a child, she felt so frustrated about this, that she had beaten and bullied her younger brother over and over again. No one not even her parents had noticed this. It was the first time she was talking about it. I told my story, too, and no one judged me in any way. It was a relief to notice that a lot more people walk around with hidden stories. The supervisor said more than once; 'Accept your past as it is, forgive yourself and others, live in the present and accept others for who they are, no more. That is enough.' 'Lucy, I've said enough now, let us order lunch and drink a glass of port to celebrate life!' 'Okay, we will go inside the restaurant, even though the weather is beautiful. It's just too windy for me outside,' Lucy said. They moved inside. A waiter walked towards them to ask in perfect English if they perhaps wanted to eat something. 'Let's sit in the corner over there.' Ann tried to sit down in a chair that was not wide enough for her big frame. But nothing could spoil her joy today. She felt as if she had lost twenty pounds, although this wasn't the case. The waiter brought the menu and asked if they wanted to have a drink first. 'Port,' Ann said: 'Half a carafe of your best Port.' 'You are not going to drink too much I hope, Ann?' 'No, of course not. I want to celebrate, that we are still together. I feel so good, I am able to sleep again!' 'I have no more nightmares, I have seen the light, it is all about peace Lucy, peace in yourself to start with. We are all in this world to learn a lesson or two. In this life I was supposed to learn that I can forgive myself, and as a result of this I can forgive others. We all are wounded mentally one way or another, one person maybe more than the other. But the essential thing in each life is to learn your lessons, and be aware of who you really are, and help others to do the same thing. Every person is unique and can contribute to the larger whole, to the purpose of existence itself.' 'Did this yogi plant these sentences in your head? Are you brainwashed or anything?' 'No, I am not. I can understand now better what the essence of my existence is. They told me the nightmare could return in one way or another. Which it did, the man turned around. He looked at me long and hard, and without words he let me know I am on the right track. I don't feel like playing hide and seek with my life a second anymore. First of all, I want to tell my story in the park to all. I am going to set up a series of lectures about my awareness and my past. I want to go back to the United Kingdom, I have a mission, there is no time to lose. 'I don't know if I will join you Ann, our life was clear and comfortable in Portugal until now. The waiter brought a carafe filled with the best port. Ann and Lucy both ordered a healthy fresh salad with tuna and almonds. Ann heard the announcement of the BBC news from a TV. In many restaurant and cafés in this part of Portugal the television was tuned to the BBC, it was standard procedure, as a service to all the British tourists. She turned her face towards the television. Lucy filled their glasses with port. 'Cheers, to a wonderful life together,' she said. 'Breaking news,' a dark lady on the screen said. 'At different places in the world terrible events took place. In the City of London, in an office, in a luxury department store in the centre of Amsterdam, at Ground Zero in the memorial centre of 9/11 in New York people suddenly fell down. It was as if they went into a coma in masses, without any apparent reason. The paramedics arrived very soon, like the police, but most of the victims were dead already. The police have done searches with dogs through every corner of the buildings at all of these different places in the world, but nothing special was found. However, the police in Amsterdam found a miniscule grey round object that was discovered in the Jewish Museum. The police (when we are informed correctly) were tipped by a foreign secret service. This object is now fully examined. It appeared in close up on television. If you see an object like this, you should immediately notify the police, guards, push the fire alarm bell and leave the building, as soon as possible. Help other people if you are capable. Call the police. The little object contains a deadly cocktail and is life threatening. It seems to spread a sort of poisonous gas and as far as we know now the object disappears after a short time. From what we know at the moment, there could be a worldwide terror network behind all of this. The press officers of all secret services we spoke do not deny nor do they confirm this. But our research department found out so far it could be the work of an Islamic terror organisation that carries the following name: ; The Dawn of the True Islam, if we are correctly informed. It seems there are different terror cells in the Netherlands, in the USA, the United Kingdom and maybe even in Northern Ireland, but we do not have all the details yet. We need to do more research. But what we do know is that a person called Samir C., a young Dutch Muslim was recently put in custody by the Dutch secret service. (the portrait of Samir C. was shown with a dash over his eyes) He is described as an excellent college student. As soon as we know more, it will be breaking news again.' Ann opened her mouth but she couldn't say a word for minutes. She almost choked in the port she still had in her mouth. She felt a sharp pain near her heart. In a split second she had to think of beautiful Donnah. 'You wanted to go back to the UK?' "What a good timing, Ann!' 'I don't think you should go, it is not safe at all over there. You never know when the next terror attack will take place with that strange object, bomb or whatever it is. This might even come from the real IRA, or some other funny Irishmen, who knows. In that case it is even more dangerous for you, with your background, please Ann, let us stay in Portugal!' 'No, I am very sorry, period.' 'It doesn't matter where you are on this earth. Danger can be anywhere. I don't want to live in fear anymore, ever again. I want to do good and love my fellow man and woman.' 'You act like a silly saint Ann, this isn't normal. Did you become more holy than father Steve this Sunday?' 'Do you want to sit next to sweet Jesus or the saints?' 'Again, I ask you in all honesty, did they brainwash you in that centre? Because I don't recognize you anymore!' 'No Lucy, I've got total awareness now, about a lot of essential matters in life. I experienced endless love, even if it was for a short period.' 'The world is collapsing and you are talking about endless love, I find it mighty strange.' 'Precisely now. Without love for each other the world will break apart totally. To answer hatred with hatred has no use, keep blaming yourself neither. I have to go to the UK, Lucy, I simply do.' 'If you can't keep me company here in Portugal, you can always visit me if you want.'

36.

Samir was taken out of his small prison cell again for interrogation. His interrogators tried to exhaust him. They hoped he would start talking in the end. During the interrogation a bright light was shining at his face. In his small cell it was never dark, day and night the lights were on, a camera watched every move. He could sleep if he wanted on a bed which was near a grey wall, the toilet was made of stainless steel and the shower was only separated from the rest of the room by a plastic curtain. Every move he made was registered. No contact was allowed with the outside world, not even his own family had permission to see him. He existed in complete isolation. Of course a few lawyers had to object to this situation, for he was kept in isolation longer than Dutch law permitted. One of them really wanted to help Samir. In one of the many tv programmes that focused on the subject of 'Terror threat from The Dawn' and 'the case Samir C.' she spoke with total disgust about how she thought Samir C. was treated. It was totally unacceptable in her eyes. Everybody had the right to speak to a lawyer, so why not Samir C.? This couldn't be tolerated and was against the constitution of the Netherlands in her opinion.

Until now Samir C. hadn't said a single word. Nothing at all. He felt very tired, hardly ate or drank anything. He was convinced his Holy Task was not over yet and he would rather die a martyr than betray 'The Dawn of True Islam'. He had no idea what was going on in the outside world. But he did know, if there had been a chance the party had begun that special Sunday. He hoped that the attacks with the poison balls had been successful. He wondered if it did happen and killed as many people as possible. The date on Sunday was carefully chosen for the first attack. This day used to be a holy day for Christians to celebrate their faith in God and Jesus Christ. But they even sold their own religious day to the devil, the shops were always open, even on Sundays, so people could buy more things they did not need, and run up their debts. That was more important than to worship God. To sell your holy day for a few coins was all there was left in the cursed western countries. But soon this world was going to be changed forever, if this had not already happened. Although he felt hungry, his spirit felt very strong. his eyes winked against the strong light which was shining in his face again. Opposite him two women in grey uniforms were seated. Two men with rifles were standing beside the door, as if this was necessary to counter some great danger… Everything in this room was white, the walls, the chairs, the table. In one wall there was a window, the glass was very thick, behind it stood a psychiatrist, a guard and an official from the Dutch secret service, the AIVD. They were observing every word and move Samir made. All the interrogation sessions were filmed and analysed afterwards, every expression in his face, every move his body made could be an indication, next to the words he spoke at last. It was no doubt that he would start talking in the end. 'Samir', one of the women said. 'We know exactly how the little poison balls work. We also know precisely where the next attacks are planned. You are working together with the 'Dawn of the True Islam' in London and New York, we know exactly who they are Samir, denial has no use at all. Tell us what you know, this may lead to a sentence that could be more lenient later on in the process. Your parents are in total grief now, they are very disappointed in you, you have hurt them very much. He closed his eyes and prayed in silence: 'Allah, oh Highest let me be brave. Oh Allah, let me do Your Will.' A very high and unpleasant sound filled the room. He opened up his eyes and said: 'Allah is the Highest, Allah is Great.' The two women looked at each other, one nodded. Nothing could be done right now to make him talk at the moment, but one of them said despite of this : 'Samir, if you cooperate with us, besides getting a lower punishment, we offer you that you may finish your education, you get special coaching and physical training as well. Your resistance has no use, we discovered all poison balls, we know their next move, you don't betray anyone. Everyone has been taken in custody already anyway. Most of the things they said wasn't true. It belonged to the method used in Samir's case, they used all sorts of psychological tricks to break his will, to exhaust him, to let him falter, without any result so far. Samir laid his head on the table, his hands around his ears. He didn't want to see or hear anything anymore. One of the women stood behind him and laid her hand on his shoulder. 'Tell us, Samir, tell us. We will help you, you can trust us.' 'Lisa, let us stop now, this has no use, let's take him to his cell for now. Maybe he can walk a little bit in the gym for a while.' Two man accompanied him to his cell. The gym, where he was allowed to walk a few rounds two times every day, consisted of a space of eight by ten yards only. The walls were white, everywhere cameras were present, with a special air circulation system fresh air came into the room. In the ceiling there were round windows with very thick glass covered by heavy steel bars, no one from either the inside or outside could ever damage this. Samir took his pillowcase from the pillow, one of the few actions he could do himself. He laid the pillowcase on the floor. He bowed his head which now touched the pillowcase for a second. He raised his arms. 'Oh Allah, please give me strength.' The door of his cell opened. Two men with guns entered his cell. 'Come with us, you get some fresh air for today.' When the door was closed behind him and the two guards Samir started walking his usual rounds, his head bowed to the floor. Suddenly he saw that one of the men had put something on the floor. He knew he'd rather not make a move, since everything was noticed, but he wondered if the sudden movement was noticed by the cameras and if any action was taken. Against all rules his guards were walking to the door and closed it, he was alone, which never happened before. He lost consciousness and fell down.

37.

'Since you agreed to work with us, we'll start immediately to get as much information from you as possible, Hannah. What exactly do you know about the 'Dawn of the True Islam and the real IRA?' 'By the way, Shalom, I am Leah. I am the one who is dealing with you in the period ahead,' she said in English with a slight American accent. Sitting next to her were a man and woman, who didn't introduce themselves. Hannah Siobhan was silent for a new moments, she had to get used to the fact they always named her Hannah. She felt a total inner alienation, now she had to talk about people with whom she had worked together for months for a higher goal. It didn't feel like betrayal to talk about them, because she felt there was now a way out, in a situation which was out of her control anyway. She had severe doubts about everything concerning her 'mission'. A camera was pointed at her, a bright light was shining in her face and a microphone stood open to record everything she was going to say in a second. 'Actually, I don't know how to start, I feel so alienated in the whole situation.' 'We understand this, it must be very strange for you. You are taken away from a very complex situation working together with the most dangerous terrorists, believing you had a mission. That is why you'll get a treatment from our psychiatrist. We want to give you more time to adjust to this new situation, but we don't have any time, it is urgent we get as much information as possible.' 'I was trained in a camp in Libya. The camp was very well equipped and set up by the 'Dawn' if I am informed correctly. The military training was professional, we were taught to handle different kinds of weapons, and we got a decent explanation about the secret weapon, this poison ball, how it worked, how to use it in different situations, with various groups. The communication with different terror cells was done by an untraceable communication system. How everything was financed I don't know exactly, but I think I heard there was a flow of money from Saudi Arabia. They didn't tell me that much, and the only reason I was allowed to take part was that the real IRA paid a large sum of money to the 'Dawn' for my training'. 'Who was it from the real IRA that knew about it all?' 'It is very difficult to talk about my contact person. I don't know if he or she is still alive and if he or she is, they will be killed for sure if they are betrayed, either by their own organisation or by MI6, no doubt about it.' 'If this person is to be found either by MI6, the CIA or by us, she or he won't be killed. The information which this person can give us is too important by far.' 'I can tell you that I had a contact person within the real IRA. She or he had contact with the 'Dawn' and was informed in a general way, but I doubt if the specific information about the poison ball was part of this, I honestly don't know.' 'What do you know about terrorist attacks that will be executed in the very near future?' 'They didn't tell me much, the less I knew the better. But I know there was a terrorist cell in Amsterdam, the name of the person I met was Samir.' We know this, did you hear anything about other plans of the 'Dawn'? 'The only thing I know is that there was contact with cells in London and New York and I assume they had plans to act in Amsterdam, too, and Rotterdam.' 'We know this.' Leah didn't tell Hannah Siobhan there had been terror attacks already and that some were prevented. She didn't want to influence Hannah in any way by giving this info. 'We end this session now, Hannah, we'll bring you back to your room, you may take a shower. If you wish to eat something and sleep, that is fine. Tomorrow at nine o 'clock you'll first have a conversation with your psychiatrist. He was educated in London, and he has worked also in Belfast for a while. He is well informed about the local circumstances, the difficult relation of all these groups within the population and the history of Ulster. I can see it in your face you are very tired. Leah put her hand on the forehead of Hannah Siobhan for a moment. 'Drink a glass of water.' The man and the women who didn't introduce themselves accompanied her to her room. They locked the door again. A meal with some fruit juce was set on the table, a little flag of Israel made the image complete. She looked at the flag, this was going to be her flag as well in the near future, she thought of the flag of Belfast with the same star, a symbol as well, she'd probably never see it again in her life. She took a sip of the fruit juice and ate something of the meal in front of her. After she laid down in the bed she fell asleep.

Her grandfather appeared in a dream, she felt deeply loved. He let her know that she was in good hands now in Israel, without any condition she could cooperate with them, her future was in this country, Israel, the land of milk and honey.

38.

'Ladies and gentlemen, in a few moments we are going to land at Heathrow Airport, please put your seat in the upright position. The weather in London is rainy and misty, it is fourteen degrees Celius. Thank you very much for flying with EasyJet, and we hope to welcome you aboard in the near future.'

'How lovely,' Ann thought: 'Oh dear, how I missed the rain, the mist and it's only fourteen degrees. How wonderful!' The temperature had been thirty degrees when she left Faro this morning. Her blouse had been totally wet from the sweat. She'd never gotten used to the high temperatures in Portugal in all those years. She zipped her coat already. Before she left she'd bought an umbrella at the Chinese store in Cacela. 'Going to the Chinese' in Portugal had nothing to do with a restaurant. You could find Chinese stores everywhere in Portugal, they sold cheap imported stuff labelled 'Made in China'. The locals as well as the tourists were very fond of the articles which could be bought there. It costed hardly anything. The Chinese in the stores spoke Portugese, but no English at all. Maybe they had come from their former colonies? Ann realized now this period was over, perhaps forever. The aircraft shook while it flew in a thick layer of grey clouds. Once beneath the clouds, you could see the green landscape of England. How she had missed this colour; green, in all its delicate varieties. In a moment she would see her sister Mandy again, finally. It had been too long since she had seen her. Ann really loved her younger sister very much. She was happily married to John, who worked at an insurance company. They had two wonderful daughters; Elizabeth and Joan. Joan studied Social Science at a college in London, Elizabeth worked as a teacher in the north of London in a difficult neighbourhood, she did her work with heart and soul. Mandy offered her a place to live in her house, which was situated in a new town, not far from London. The house had four bedrooms, two of them were not occupied because Elizabeth and Joan both didn't live at home anymore. Mandy had told Ann in a long telephone conversation she could stay as long as she wanted to, in fact she'd love this. Ann told Mandy she had to fulfill a special mission in Great Britain, the one of reconciliation. In the opinion of Mandy this was almost an impossible task in todays' Britain. After the recent terror attacks there had been announced the so called Code Red, an alarm code that was given out by the government. Everywhere the British army was present, on every corner, in every street. An emergency law was introduced, the police had the authority to search anyone without having to give a reason for this. This led to tension in the large Muslim communities in the country. They protested because, in their view, Muslims were now the victims of this discriminating policy. As if the police had a legal excuse to control and observe them constantly and everywhere. In a news item an imam said he was very worried that everybody thought that behind every Muslim was a terrorist monster, hidden but ready to strike at the unbelievers.

Ann went on and on to convince her sister it was now the right time to preach about reconciliation. 'You'll see Ann, what is going on here now when you will get here,' Mandy had said at the end of the long telephone conversation. The plane landed, in a moment she would see and embrace her sister. The door was opened by a steward. She grabbed her luggage. Slowly a row of people started to walk to the exit. Ann thanked the stewardesses for a very pleasant flight and walked through the corridor, in the direction of the conveyor belt that would bring the suitcases. She noticed the police and men of the British army were present everywhere. It was as if she'd landed in a police state. They all carried automatic weapons. She picked up her suitcase from the belt, but she could not walk through customs as usual. Everyone had to answer questions, suitcases had to be opened to be checked, she had to empty her handbag completely. But that was not all, she had to remove her shoes and go to through a thorough body check, what a welcome to her own country! Even though the sign was green, they frisked her anyway. She felt awkward and totally surprised by all of this. Finally she could pass and embrace her sister, who was waiting for her.

39.

The Dutch press found out that Samir C. died in prison. No explanation was given as to why he had died, and under which circumstances. Different experts talked about it at length in news items. A psychiatrist said perhaps he had committed suicide as a result of the solitary confinement, and the aggressive interrogation methods used. Another expert, a retired police officer said that the guards had slept. They had not noticed how bad the condition of the young man was. In his opinion the interrogation team exhausted Samir C. by the treatment they gave him every day. The opinion of a well-known lady lawyer was that the Dutch secret service should be investigated, that a young man had died like he did was too serious not to investigate. The parents of Samir C. had to start a procedure against the Dutch state and make a claim for all the damage they'd suffered. But not only this, human rights in general were at stake here. A very serious fact by any standard. The Dutch secret service was asked to comment but they refused to do this in front of the camera. In a note they wrote :

'We regret the sudden unexpected death of Samir C. We don't know how this could happen. We will investigate this very carefully.'

The prime minister, Mrs. Toorop, only wrote a short note that this whole matter was now a subject of a scrupulous investigation. The leaders of all political parties were not permitted to speak about the case of Samir C. in any way on radio, television, or in the newspapers. A lot of journalists protested against this, it was against the freedom of speech. To them it was a dangerous sign, the liberties of democracy were at stake itself, they were very worried about these developments. The foreign press had settled down in big vans in front of the building of the AIVD, near The Hague. The whole day they made up news items that were not to be found at that location itself. They filled their programmes with experts who gave their opinion over and over again. The image which was given about the Dutch secret service was one of a small and clumsy organisation that didn't even know what happened inside its own walls.

Every Dutch newspaper opened with 'the case of Samir C.' every day, as if there was no other news anymore from the rest of the world. In newspaper articles different analyses were given, this depended on which analyst gave his or her opinion. A historian wrote that the Dutch stupidity knew literally no borders at all. He said that the Dutch were not aware that this dangerous international terrorist organisation had infiltrators in many layers of the society. That much more would happen in the near future. This organisation was very professional, with advanced technology probably and acute knowledge of different societies, they knew very well whom to recruit for their organisations, ready to hit any democracy in the heart. This democracy (according to the historian) was under great pressure now, no doubt about it. A famous psychiatrist said that any new recruit could be totally brainwashed by a terror group. Even death had another meaning to them, it was not the end of life but a new beginning in Paradise. She also warned against mass hysteria given the whole situation a lot of countries in Western Europa were in. You never knew when the next attack would take place. Only a few politicians of the right wing party, who did speak to media even though it was strictly forbidden, said it was Samir C.'s own fault he had died. One of them ended his comment with ; 'Nicely taken to an end of his sorry life, we don't need such people in our country anyway.' The Islamic community remained largely silent. It was as if there was an agreement among them not to speak or react at all in public. Photos were published of the brother, sister and parents of Samir C. without permission. This was very unpleasant for them, one could imagine. Their privacy was rudely violated in every way. The photo's appeared in magazines, tabloids and right wing newspapers. Their lawyer announced on television she would sue all who had published the pictures. Over and over again a deep investigation about the mysterious death of Samir C. was promised in the media. Why wasn't Samir C. discovered earlier on? Was it because he had been selected to meet the queen at the elderly home? Nothing was found at the time, nothing that could be held against him. The king and queen were not commenting on anything, of course. They were kept away from the press in these difficult circumstances. Their safety was a matter of great concern to everybody involved. After a few weeks Mrs. Toorop, the prime minister, held a speech on national television. The idea was that perhaps she could calm down the nation. She said that the secret services of different countries were working together very closely. She said the state did everything in its power to guarantee the safety of all citizens of the Netherlands. She hoped that all understood not every Muslim is a terrorist. She ended her speech with the words: 'Go to sleep gently, we will watch over your safety.'

Two weeks later at a heavily guarded meeting in the Jewish Museum in Amsterdam, another poison ball attack was a fact. There were no casualties, but sixty people had to be evacuated and treated at a hospital. They had 'severe health problems to be looked after,' the officials said. The secret service had no idea how this attack could happen. They had been thinking that they had rooted out all of the groups. Their comment was the usual soothing one: 'We are going to find out why this happened in a deep investigation.' Again, they had no other mantra.

40.

The training camp in Libya was traced. Hannah Siobhan had been of great help to locate the camp. The decision was made to destroy the camp with so called smart bombs that could do the job very precisely. The Israeli government cooperated with the Pentagon, the American government and its defence specialists. Of course the presidents of both countries communicated regularly with each other, almost every day now. The Israeli air force struck hard, and nothing was left of the camp. The media found out immediately after the bombing took place. Some journalists called it; 'Another aggressive action of the state of Israel against the poor and oppressed Arabs.' Others commented this action was more than necessary, because the world was living in insecurity and fear. The poison ball attacks needed a firm response. The analysts in the newspapers made many speculations. This was maybe the beginning of a new world order. The world would never be the same anymore. You could never know when the next attack with the poison ball would take place, nor if it really was an attack since the little balls vanished after they had been used. Nobody was safe anymore. It had not been discovered yet in which countries exactly the terrorist cells operated, some doubted if it was even possible to discover all of them. It seemed like the balls were produced at different places around the world, and then distributed in secret. Western European countries like the Netherlands, Great Britain, France, Belgium, Germany upgraded the level of terror threat every week. The armies in those countries were mobilized, it was always present at strategic sites, and sometimes they operated undercover. Troops were recalled from missions overseas. Royal families were protected in an almost absurd way. Even their own private staff was not trusted anymore, after some moles were discovered there, too. Before the staff was allowed to enter the private quarters they had to go through checks, like undressing themselves completely every day. Schools in most western European countries looked more like prisons with all security checks, guards, police with dogs and special armed forces walking around. In some Dutch schools riots took place, Islamic students fought with young native Dutch citizens. One group felt discriminated against, and was very angry about what had happened to Samir C. while he was in prison. The other group hated the Islamic students who were all potential terrorists in their view. In some neighbourhoods ethnic group fighting broke out. Riots were everywhere, not just in Holland but also in other Western European countries. Prime ministers and heads of state begged the media to 'show some responsibility, for the safety of the nation, and not to report on every tiny incident'.

Hannah S. was permitted to watch the news again. She had the intensive psychotherapy behind her now. This special treatment became less intensive bit by bit. The psychiatrist had noticed she had a good capacity to adapt to a new situation, mentally she was not ill, but quite intelligent. Hannah S. discovered in therapy that she had never felt safe in the neighbourhood in Belfast where she grew up. Emotional issues of her father had reflected on her. They had had a deep impact on her own development as a child. He never had been able to really protect her, because of his own sorrow inside. She spoke about her feelings of complete loneliness in the training camp in Libya. The psychiatrist confronted her with the sudden changes in her life, this shouldn't be underestimated. They were bound to have a deep impact on her life for a longer period. While she was still having these conversation and under severe monitoring of the Mossad, she had learned Modern Hebrew very fast in a special programme. Bit by bit she entered the Israeli society, a visit to a shop to test her language skills, a visit to the beach near Tel Aviv, were already possible, but she was never alone. There was always someone of the Mossad at her side. Her new identity of 'Hannah Daran' became more real to her every day. She got precise instructions how to behave in different situations, what to tell or not to tell, what to say and what not to say. This was all part of becoming a citizen of Israel. The education system of the country was explained to her, she had to do a test, and she passed. The purpose was that her cover as a teacher would become complete. The Mossad wished not just for that reason alone that Hannah S. were to work in Israeli society. This was also psychologically better for her, to have a basis in life and to fully integrate. Any person was more stable that way, the Mossad couldn't use mentally instable persons as an informant. As a preparation for her future job as a teacher copies of her diplomas were made, but these were showing her new name. However, her place of birth remained the city of Belfast. The work was done in an excellent way, no one would ever discover the papers weren't real ones. She did not ask how they had done this, she knew by now the usual answer would be: 'It is a state secret, so it is classified information.' Just like her new passport was.

A few months later the Mossad announced it was time to apply for a job, she was ready for it. She was ready, too, to move into a small apartment in Tel Aviv. The furnishing and rent was paid by the Mossad via an account that she had access to as well. She now was able to transfer money to her own account for every day expenses. On the opposite of her apartment Tal moved in. He had a simple job in a kiosk at the boulevard, near the beach as a cover for his work as an informant. He was there for Hannah S. and was there for her safety. He kept an eye on her, and reported about her to the Mossad every week. If she felt not safe for one reason or another she could always ask Tal for help. He called her often for a chat.

The apartment was furnished in a modern style. The furniture was all of one colour, a soft white just like the very luxurious modern kitchen and the bathroom at the back. Her bedroom had an open closet, a comfortable bed. It was equipped with a large desk and a computer. The walls were bare. She got the permission to buy some reproductions of paintings, little things to make the place a bit more personal. At first she had asked if she could have a poster of the cliffs of Moher to put on the empty wall. This wasn't permitted, it was strictly forbidden to refer to the Republic of Ireland in any way. She felt very disappointed and had to realize very sharply her life had limitations, probably forever.

So instead she put up three reproductions of paintings by Monet on the wall. One showed a beautiful woman beneath a parasol with light bright colours, the second one had water lilies in an intense green, she loved this painting very much. The third one showed a breezy Dutch landscape with a windmill, near a river.

After she applied for a teaching job twice, she was invited for an interview. Tal gave her the last tips, how she could present herself in the very best way. He wished her a lot of success. She was lucky and got the job. Eighteen hours of teaching, very nice to start with. She was also asked if she wanted to participate in a project in which the lessons were given in English. She was willing to do this of course, her new life got another shape again. Still, she was worried very much about her parents, and asked more than once if it was permitted to have be in touch with them. This was not to be: they told her that her parents knew she was safe and sound, but they did not give any particulars as to how and why. The usual answer was given again, she could dream the wording. A sentence she would never forget anymore ; 'It is a state secret, and this is classified information, so we are sorry we cannot give it to you.' Every week she had a meeting with Leah, who remained her contact person at the Mossad. The contact had been constructive and positive from both sides until now. She wrote a log on a daily basis, every memory of the Islamic terror organisation was written down, as detailed as possible. To speak about the real IRA and Sean was still very difficult for her. It was emotionally too heavy. She wondered sometimes where Sean could be now and if he was still alive, she never heard anything from him anymore since she had had to leave Portugal in the way she had done.

41.

The safety measures in the UK were increased to an even higher level. Terror code red, which was the highest level so far was not enough. The government introduced an extra code. It was 'terror code white', an extreme code. This new code had an immense impact on everyday public life. The army was present at every corner in the streets, day and night. At every public building tanks and other armoured vehicles were present. Their grumbling engines could be heard at odd times, when they moved from one spot to the other. At every school there were at least five guards, walking through the buildings day and night, every student was searched when entering the school. They had to go through detection gates and every bag had to be emptied to show its contents. If there was the slightest indication that something was wrong, a student was picked out of the row for further interrogation. Some newspapers wrote about this; they said it was outrageous to treat teens and children like this and they stated that Muslim and black students were checked more often and more strict than white students. According to the papers this would only have the result that society would become more unstable, and as it was the situation was already bad, very bad. The British parliament had become a fortress now, its open and democratic atmosphere was a thing of the past. Fear was felt everywhere in society since a new incident took place. Ann Pigden, the lady activist for reconciliation between the British and Irish peoples, had a full house again. With a lot of passion she told her own story of the British army and its actions during Bloody Sunday. She talked at great length of her discovery: that suppressing the past gave no inner peace. She advised people to confront oneself with it, get aware of your own role, and open up to your former enemy and start a dialogue and the process of reconciliation. In this way everyone who really wanted could contribute to peace on earth, in our days. You will surely experience that your enemy is human, just like yourself, made of flesh and blood. The British press noticed her after some time. She had an interview on national television and radio. A newspaper had a very long interview with her. They called her 'A brave woman, a beacon of hope in turbulent times, she contributed to establish a better future for all mankind.' But alas, Ann was no more. She was in a big hall filled with people, they had all died together, during one of her lectures. Of course the authorities thought right away a poison ball had done its devastating work again. Everybody in the public domain reacted horrified. How on earth could this have happened? With so many checkpoint, police, guards and police dogs walking around? Ann and her audience were seen as a target by the officials, so there had been the usual security measures. Again they were faced with a fait accompli.

Her funeral was covered live by the BBC. It was held in the Westminster Abbey. The prime minister and the queen were sitting in the front row. Ann's sister gave an emotional speech. Lucy was too emotional to say one word, let alone give a speech. All the people present were singing 'God save the Queen'. Father Steve had conducted the ceremony, at the request of Lucy. Jeff was representing the park, dressed smartly for the occasion. At the park they organized a memorial for Ann, where she had become a hero, almost a saint, not only to them but a symbol for Great Britain as well, a proud country that now seemed to be on the verge of collapse. During the ceremony people held each other's hand.

The government announced another thorough investigation concerning her death, but the population didn't believe a word anymore about this investigation or that. More and more it was said out aloud that people who did not have a British background should leave the country for once and for all. This voice soon became a new political party, 'The United Kingdom, solely for its own people'. Although the houses of parliament were still heavily guarded the discussions inside didn't stop. Other opinions were heard, too. Democracy had not been murdered yet. It did not die that easily, the people knew it well.

42.

The daily routine of getting up, packing her bag for school, look into her lessons for the last time, to make lunch, had given Hannah S. a grip on her life to a certain extent. She taught history and a few hours at the English Department of a small 'middle school'. All students attended this type of education, three years before they went to high school. The Mossad had chosen an ordinary school, not an international private school, this could attract attention, you never knew which students would enrol. They could be from foreign families or children of diplomats. The most important thing was to let her play a role as normally as possible in Israeli society. For her colleagues at school she was Hannah, a woman with compassion for her students, who spoke Modern Hebrew excellently, who had a decent knowledge of the subject she was teaching. She really helped to set up the English department of the school. Still, she kept everyone at a distance emotionally, she was afraid to make new friends. Sometimes she had a drink with a female colleague at weekends. But she felt down, no matter what she did. She had mentioned this to her psychiatrist, but she couldn't really help her, but mentioned that she suffered from suppressed mourning. She had lost so many things, the presence of her family, her life in Ireland with its own habits and climate, her youth in Belfast of which she couldn't speak to anyone now. It still was part of her identity, always deeply hidden inside. If you deny mourning and you can't share it with other people, one way or another this will come to the surface, one way or another, according to the psychiatrist. She encouraged Hannah S. to talk about it as much as she could in their sessions. She prescribed anti-depressiva, not only for the wellbeing of Hannah S. but also because the Mossad had no use for a depressed person. After a few weeks she felt a bit better. But she realized in a painful way she had always played a role. There was always a gap between her and the outside world. This world consisted of the modern state of Israel. What really helped her was her contact with her students. Children were in the age between twelve and fifteen, so they were in their puberty if they lived in Israel, Belfast, London or Amsterdam, they went through the same phase in life. Sometimes they could react already in an adult way, but in another situation they might react as children. Sometimes they were only busy with their outlooks. Hannah S. loved those kids, be it in Israel or anywhere else. Those kids gave her a sort of stability in life. When she was teaching or helping them in the classroom she totally forgot in which situation she was, and lived in the here and now. This moved her inside, in spite of the anti-depressiva she took. She also loved the modern and vibrant atmosphere of Tel Aviv. The wonderful boulevards, the beach, the trendy shops, the magnificent museum of art and the parks. When she was at one of these sites she felt anonymous, one of the crowd. This felt as a liberation for a while, as if life finally became normal again. This never lasted long. Sometimes she was called in for a conversation with Leah as a result of another attack, an unforeseen happening on the world scene. When she was at work she had to sign out as soon as possible when her task at school was finished. This gave her the feeling she'd never belong to herself any more.

Today it was her 'homework' day. She logged in to the system of the school; its name was Ofri. The school had one of the most modern systems in the country. The students were not only graded by letters and figures, the whole development as a person mattered. She did not only like this kind of education, but she felt proud as a teacher to function in it. It made her look at her students in a different way. But this was not all, she was developing herself in this manner as well. The past never let go of her. Last Sunday she had to sign in. In the conversation that followed with Leah, it became clear that Ann Pigden and a large number of people had been killed, the cause was probably one of the poison balls. This came as a shock to Hannah S. Now the woman she had wanted to kill was dead. Leah warned her this would be in the news over and over again. The Mossad had a hunch that the real IRA was still active and working together with the 'Dawn of the True Islam', this might be the result of it. Hannah had to tell very precisely what she did know about the real IRA.

She looked outside, it was a beautiful day and she felt like going to the beach instead of working at her computer all day. The bell of her apartment rang. This hardly ever happened. She picked up the horn of the intercom. 'Shalom, it's me, David, can I come up?' She didn't answer but pushed the button to open up the door to the stairs. Footsteps came closer, she opened the door and fell in David's arms. 'I missed you', he said.' 'I missed you terribly when I had the time,' she said smiling. 'Hannah, I must say I have permission to see you but… because of safety reasons I can't say anymore,' Hannah ended his sentence. She pulled him into the bedroom. They made love passionately, no pills no thoughts, no sorrow separated her from this other human being, David, blessed be his name.

43.

Hannah S. asked Leah if it was permitted to tell David more about her personal life story. She got used to asking for permission, also about private matters. It seemed like it had become her second nature, she was afraid to express herself spontaneously. After consulting the psychiatrist she came to the conclusion that it was permitted, but only in the connection with David, and for the time being. Very slowly she could let go a bit of her frozen outside, her cold outer skin. David was not only a loving person towards her, he also had a lot of patience with her. To make more contact with her real feelings her psychiatrist suggested she'd start to play the violin. This turned out to be the golden idea, music is an emotional expression that needs no words. They provided a good violin. For Hannah S. it meant when she played her violin, that in her concentration she felt liberated from the limitations of her current life. She really loved to play with others. In different groups she had played all sorts of music, pop, jazz, and yiddish music. She was a fast learner. She was allowed to meet David's family and his friends. This gave her a feeling that she belonged somewhere, but more so, she felt welcome. Especially in the contact with Ruth, David's mother, who was a retired psychologist who had mostly dealt with kids. She had worked at several schools. Now and then she still had a consultation at home, in special cases she'd love to help children with behaviour disorders. Although she always missed her own mother, Ruth gave Hannah the feeling there was a mother figure in her life now. Ruth introduced her to one of her friends, the violin player Max Rothfeld. Max offered to give her violin-lessons. Hannah S. was very glad with his offer, and so she accepted this. Max directly noticed her natural feeling for music, in no time, just by hearing, she learned to play all kinds of music. He invited her to play in a music group which was specialized in different kind of yiddish music with European roots from Hungary, Portugal and Poland. The group practised twice a week with a singer, Naomi. When playing her violin with the others she closed her eyes. In her imagination she saw the green hills around Dingle, the little stream of Spancil Hill. Although the kind of music she played now was quite different from the Irish traditional, the intense feeling of totally losing yourself while playing was exactly the same.

Max asked the group to play at a festival of the 'Peace now' movement. They expected a lot of people on the 'Square of Peace'. Hannah had asked Leah for permission to take part in this event. Leah consulted a few people within the Mossad. They gave her permission to play at the concert.

Hannah was very excited, she told David: 'David, imagine, I am going to play for thousands of people in Israel at a peace festival!' 'I never thought I would enjoy playing my violin again. 'The one who doesn't believe in miracles, is no realist in the land of Israel,' David quoted Ben Gurion, smiling broadly.